ARMY OF DARKNESS
OMNIBUS

Gold Edition

I0676919

Army of Darkness Omnibus: Gold Edition
Copyright © 2014 Andrew James Cooper
Published by Realms of Varda
www.vardabooks.com

All Rights Reserved. No part of this book may be reproduced, scanned, or distributed in any print or electronic form without permission.

All characters appearing in this work are fictitious. Any resemblance to real persons, living or dead, is purely coincidental.

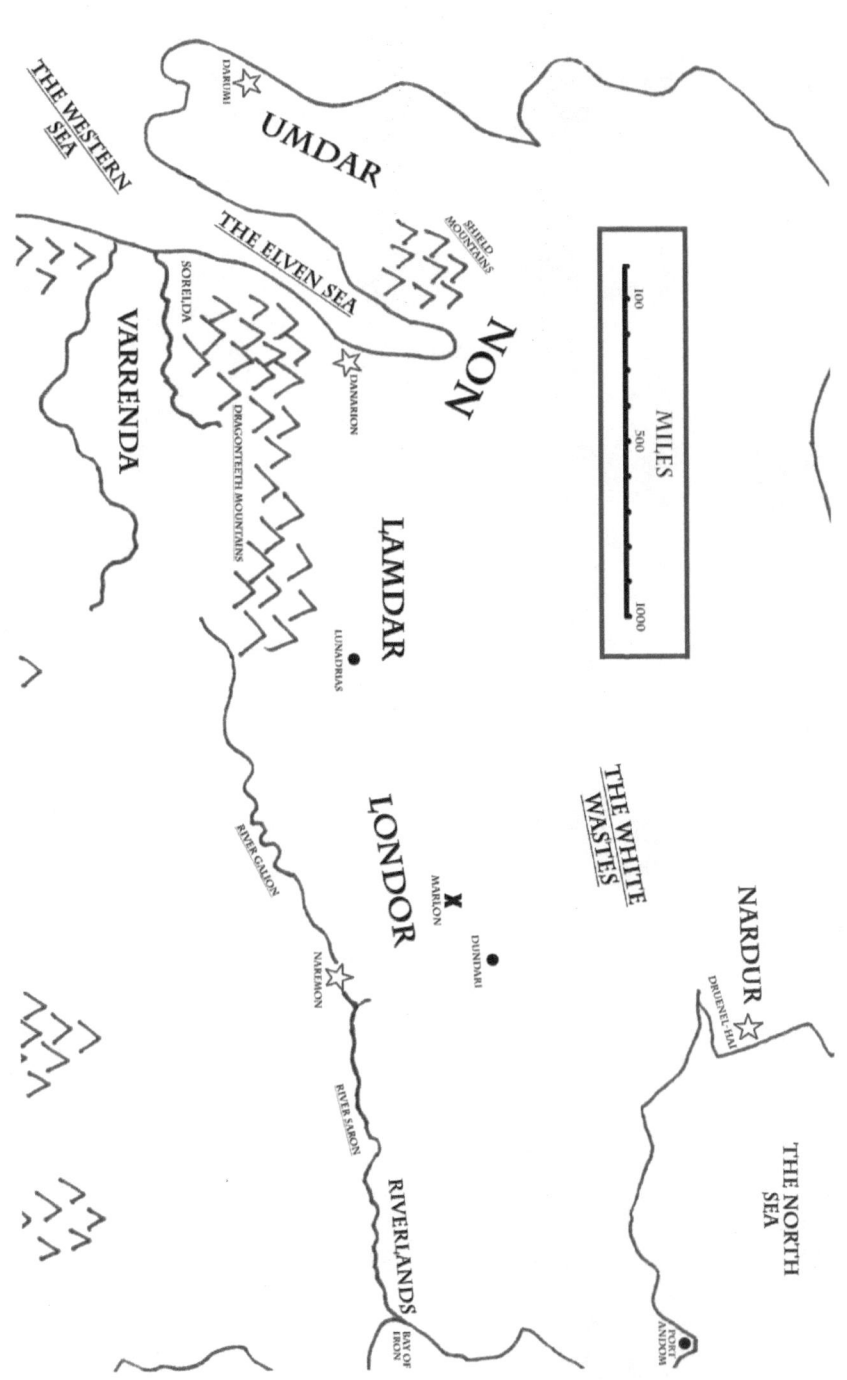

TABLE OF CONTENTS

ARMY OF DARKNESS

CHAPTER ONE

Indryas, son of Narsoli and Admé

Murder, though Indryas had seen a lot of it, was hard to stomach. Matricide, even harder. But his uncle Shakes (a more fitting name than Sarsoli) didn't seem very bothered about Grandmother's death at breakfast.

The balding, seventy-year-old elf clutched his spoon with an ever-trembling hand. His eyes had a wilder look than they normally did. He looked hungry, but not for food.

Indryas was sitting in the Hall of Feasting with his family: his cousins Sarsi and Sarsé (children of Uncle Shakes); his brother Drusion; his half-sister Ari; and a collection of nieces and nephews, smacking as they ate and yelling, whom Indryas grew to hate more and more every day.

The breakfast was prepared as well as it ever had been: the slaves had given Indryas a generous dollop of almond pudding, steamed apples, wheatcakes drizzled in honey, and a bowl of raspberries. But nothing he ate satisfied him. He needed something more.

Indryas looked around at his family. They looked unsettled, like him. Something was wrong. *Something happened last night. Something changed. But what?*

Grandfather Gilden, sitting at the head of the table, had stopped eating altogether. A frown had fallen over his pitted grey face; and there was something in his ruddy eyes that Indryas did not like.

The slaves had gathered in the feasting hall, waiting for the family to finish their breakfast. Their eyes were shallow, afraid; even they knew something was wrong.

Uncle Shakes stood up.

"Can I help you, master?" a slave said.

It all unraveled in an instant. Uncle Shakes had teeth—huge

white teeth the size of fingers—and he had sunk them into the slave's fragile neck; he was moaning in ecstasy as he drank from her blood. Gilden's eyes, seeing this, had widened with desire and, now, he was racing across the room with bulging white fangs. The slaves were screaming. The family had abandoned their breakfast for darker fare.

Indryas leapt out of his seat and ran.

~

By dusk, the people of Marlon—capital of the province—had either fled or died at the hands of Indryas' family. Sarsi, Sarsé, and Uncle Shakes had been the worst of the lot, glutting themselves on blood like savage animals. Indryas refused to take part. Why, he didn't know. The violence and irreligion of Grandfather already destroyed their respect among the other elven nations. Still, though he hungered, it didn't seem right.

At a balcony, he stared at the city and the sea of pines that surrounded it. He had a feeling the King would not stand for this; they had tolerated much, but this massacre would be inexcusable. Indryas' family hadn't acted wisely... in their mad bloodlust, they failed to shut the gate and prevent escape. Now a hundred blabbering mouths ran in every direction. Word would spread. It might be a week before the King's armies arrived, but word would spread.

~

The silence of the following morning felt uneasy. Without slaves, how would they manage? Indryas had a feeling that Grandfather would not tarry long; they could not function without help.

At the sun's first rays, Drusion—brother and chamber-mate— stirred as well. He looked different: whiter, harsher-featured, bloodthirsty.

"Brother," Indryas greeted him.

Drusion did not reply for a while. He shielded his eyes from the light. "Bright, isn't it," he muttered.

"Did you partake?" The question surprised him, though it came from his own lips.

"Of course. Why wouldn't I?" Drusion stood up. "Ah, no slaves to dress me. How will I function? I drank Lunesti dry. Now, I will never look presentable."

"You could dress yourself," Indryas suggested.

Drusion snarled. The sound was more lupine than elven. "You're a year my elder, Indryas, but don't expect to inherit anything. We saw you standing there, not drinking, pious like some god-fearer. The family hated you before, but now I'd be careful about your safety, brother."

And now, with my condition, the wider world will hate me, too.

In the throne room of Gilthon Castle, one of Indryas' nieces—Lorlé, by name—had donned her black robe. The snake across center, embroidered in gold thread, gave Indryas unwelcome reminders of the Great War that had gone on so many years ago. Who knew why Gilden had summoned Lorlé, initiated antipriest and devotee of the Dark One? His forces had been defeated, though Lorlé claimed that His influence remained, that His cause was not lost, that He would one day return and win the "Forever War."

"My dearest Lorlé," Grandfather said, "a change has come over us all. You are the beloved of the Dark One. You must know His purposes for this."

"The purposes of the antigod are not immediately known." Her eyes were uncertain.

Is she hiding something, or does she simply not know, Indryas wondered.

But Grandfather's patience had run thin. "If you do not know the purposes of the antigod, how can you call yourself His servant?"

In an instant, Lorlé became talkative. "Yes, yes, Great-Grandfather. I do know. I *am* his servant." He had done worse things than kill his offspring. He had killed his wife, after all. "He has given us a great gift. He has given us the desire for blood because... because..."

She is floundering. Indryas almost had pity on her.

"Because it makes us strong!"

Grandfather's frown did not vanish. "A useless girl, you are. I want the truth, Lorlé. And if you do not give me the truth, your fate will be worse than Grandmother's. If you lie, I will know."

"Great-Grandfather." Lorlé eyed the floor. "Antipriests do not know the will of the Dark Father straightaway. I must devote myself, make sacrifices, and—"

"What do you know? I can read your dishonesty." Grandfather's voice was like thunder. "You aren't telling me everything. You *will*, if you know what is best for you. I suspect blood-drinkers will taste just as good as slaves."

"Last night I had a dream. It said the gods cursed you for killing Grandmother and... other things... and they cursed all your seed as well. Great-Grandfather, you can't let this anger you—"

"*Silence!*" Grandfather shouted. "The gods planted a dream in your head, Lorlé. That can mean one thing. Your mind is not dark. You do not serve the Dark One. You are a false antipriest. Moreover, you are a spy."

"Lies!" The accusation had filled Lorlé's eyes with zeal. "I despise the gods. I am an antipriest, and—"

The backhanded strike from Grandfather sent her into the floor with a thump. "I condemn you to die. You are not my granddaughter. I command my family to drink. When her blood is gone, we will toss her in the streets with the rest of the rabble."

Immediately, they attacked her. *How quickly we turn on our own.* If Indryas did not partake, he would face a similar fate. Grandfather had no mercy, and there was little pattern to his cruelty. Indryas raced over, bowling Drusion to the side, and sank his jaws into Lorlé's arm. The high as the blood rushed into Indryas' gums filled him with an ecstasy greater than anything he had ever felt, more pleasurable than the most sumptuous nine-course feast or any slave he had ever bedded. He knew he would not resist next time; he'd do it again, and again, and again.

~

In late afternoon, a rider came galloping through Marlon's open gates. Darrias was a thin elf of less than fifty years. His long blond hair and grass-green eyes were typical of the do-gooder Lamen tribe that Grandfather despised, but young Darrias served Gilden as a spy in one of the far-flung outposts. He served the "evil pretender," Prince Gilden, not out of any devotion to the Dark One or any real loyalty. Nay, his motivation was purely gold and silver; but even the promise of reward failed to keep the fear from his eyes as he rode among the bloodless white corpses strewn about the road.

Indryas wondered if he should warn him to stay away, but that seemed foolish even for the biggest "do-gooder" among Gilden's family. If Grandfather could not control himself, then Darrias would get a well-deserved punishment for treachery. *There is the piety, again. I must control myself.* Indryas smirked.

~

Grandfather met Darrias at the gates of Gilthon Castle. His dark purple robe and silver belt contrasted starkly with Darrias' bright oranges and reds. The iron crown Grandfather wore had been designed as the opposite of the true king's sun-and-stars gold circlet: its somber gray spikes made one think of war, not summer and beauty.

Grandfather gazed at Darrias until he spoke.

"My lord," he said, "word of the massacre has spread everywhere. Some of the survivors are hiding out in Lunadrias."

The fortress was far away, but Grandfather's thirst for bloodshed knew no distance.

"That does not matter." Darrias panted, out of breath. "The King has already marshaled a great army. It has already departed Danarion, and the leader is a great sorceress. They are making for Marlon. There are thirty, perhaps forty, thousand soldiers. I would suggest you leave."

Grandfather's eyes hardened. "You are a bearer of information, not an advisor. Do not presume to lecture me, Darrias. Your information will not go unrewarded. You may have your life."

Darrias bit his lip. He knew his vulnerable position, though Indryas could tell the lack of payment angered him. *He risked his life for gold, and now he is disappointed.* "My lord." His soft tone could not conceal a caustic edge. "I am afraid I require further payment."

"Get out," Grandfather said. "I have no use for you anymore. Believe me, if you look around, you will see that keeping your life is a great gift; and in truth, it is better than you deserve."

"My lord," Darrias growled. His hand went to his sword and then drew back.

Grandfather let his fangs show and hissed.

Darrias' bladder emptied. He whimpered, wheeled his horse around, and galloped off the way he had come.

~

At dinner, Grandfather announced his plans to one and all. His thirty progeny listened with eager ears, and an ever-present bit of fear. "My family. The King of the West has sent an army toward us. Even in all our strength and newfound gifts, we cannot stand against an army of forty thousand. The people of Marlon are dead and we cannot defend the walls ourselves."

In some ways Grandfather was mad, but he often made sense.

"Our greatest subject is Dundari. It has some soldiers and impregnable walls."

Dundari, frontier town, Queen of the Great White North, was in the furthermost inhabited land. The ancient dwarves, in the time before their fall, had constructed its walls. It was impregnable indeed. *Yes, Grandfather does make sense sometimes.*

"It is a seven days' journey by horse." Grandfather smiled, rare occasion that it was. "We will stop at towns along the way, and make use of whatever provisions and *people* they contain."

Ari threw back her head and laughed, and her silken black hair glinted in the Feasting Hall's light.

His smile vanished, perhaps at Ari's laugh. "An army of many thousands is mighty, but it is slow. If we get to Dundari, we will have shelter for the winter. The Lamen will not deal well with such weather. They know nothing of frostbite or impassible roads. They will give up in time; the King of the West will make peace with me, and we will return to Marlon. The King of the West is weak, as are his subjects. They prefer peace to war, as all do; but they prefer it overmuch. He will threaten, but he will do nothing. No doubt he learned his weak ways from my father."

At times, Indryas forgot that his own great-grandfather was once King of the West. Danthemari and his son Gilden could not have been more different. Where one had been pious, the other despised piety. Where one had respected the people, the other took slaves. Where one had worshiped the gods with unbridled devotion, the other served the Dark One with zeal.

They departed at dusk. In his new state, the dark of night did not seem to faze Indryas, and sleep seemed an unnecessary diversion. It seemed his family felt the same way; they continued well into the night.

Throughout it all, Indryas could see perfectly. The road leading north was packed dirt, unlike the paved thoroughfares that crisscrossed Londor's network of cities and eventually took you to Lunadrias, the easternmost do-gooder outpost. No, the road north was ill cared-for, and they did not bother to light it with star-gems. The north was a barren place, sparsely-populated and fruitless for the King. Only Dundari, Queen of the Great White North, had any semblance of culture. And winter was coming.

CHAPTER TWO

Drusion, son of Narsoli and Admé

Drusion had never liked the north. In fact, Marlon was too cold for him already, and Dundari promised to be far worse. As a boy, he spent a few years as a page, serving in the court of King Danthemari just as the cracks were starting to appear, as the world as they knew it was coming undone. Drusion had fled as the Great War broke out; always one step ahead, he escaped Danarion, the capital, just as Grandfather announced he had sided with the Dark One. It had been a horrible time for him, for everyone, even before the war broke out; but at least it was warm, and, even in the dead of winter, it never snowed.

They continued in the dark of the night. Grandfather was mad, yes, but at least he had the sense to flee from a forty-thousand strong army. He was bold and reckless, yes, and mad, but no one could accuse him of stupidity. After all, he had survived this long after a life of depravity, escaping the swords and staves of the "do-gooders," as he liked to call him; some might say two-hundred and seven years was more than he deserved.

A wolf howled as the thirty of them hurried down the road. Another piercing howl followed. The wolves north of Marlon were larger than most, hungrier and quicker to prey on elves, but they had no time to be afraid.

~

As the sun dawned, casting beams of rosy light through the pine boughs, a settlement appeared. Drusion wasn't foolish enough to think it would be a peaceful visit. The villagers gathering water at the well fell down, prostrate, before their tyrant. Their reverence and fear would not be enough. Uncle Shakes hopped off his horse first and scrambled after a village woman. Judging by the terror in her eyes, she knew something bad was coming, but not exactly what.

At the sight of Uncle Shakes' fangs sunk into her frail white neck, Drusion's own began to protract. Even if he felt any kind of guilt—which he didn't—Grandfather punished "do-goodedness" severely.

As Drusion found his own blood meal, he saw that Indryas had stayed back. *His piety will be the end of him.* He gave a thought to his only full brother, who he perhaps loved.

~

The seven-day journey lasted eight; on the seventh, a heavy snow began to fall. The road became difficult to discern. It struck Drusion that they had truly come to the edge of the world. The maps ended at Dundari, Queen of the Great White North.

But at last they found her, in the afternoon of the eighth day. The walls stretched forty feet in the air, as strong as they were tall: light yellow in color, with griffin statues along the posts and a few silhouettes—archers—standing on the battlements. Beside the small city, and probably within, hot springs exhaled vapor above the scraggly pines. Wood benches surrounded them, but there were no bathers in sight. It seemed everyone had gone inside the city. And the gates were shut.

Drusion couldn't shake an ominous feeling. But Grandfather took the lead, riding forward in front of the massive gate.

"Beloved subjects! May the Dark One bless you!"

They still worship the gods, even if they don't tell you. Drusion bit his lip.

"Your lord requires shelter!" Grandfather said. "His enemies are near."

"Indeed, they are." As Drusion's eyes focused, the shape of Darrion, ruler of the city, distinguished itself: a heavy set elf with white-blond hair and silvery eyes, wearing a fur coat. "Your enemies are within my city, in fact. Your enemies are standing on the walls. Your enemies, 'Lord' Gilden, are everyone except you!"

"Lies!" Ari hissed.

"Quiet, Ari." Grandfather's composure was surprising. "I command you to open the gates of Dundari, as your prince."

"And I refuse it." Darrion spoke with equal calm. "You are my king no longer. I have joined with King Danirias, and pledged myself to the true ruler. Word of your evil has spread to the Great White North, Gilden, and I know what will happen if I open my gates to you. I stood idly by while you served the Dark One, gave you lip-service for the sake of peace. But I, unlike you, care about my subjects; and I will not let a monster into my gates."

"Let me in."

Why is Grandfather so calm?

"I fear you will be very disappointed with the results if you disobey me. *Open the gates.*"

"Never." Darrion's voice quivered slightly. "Gilesti Danirias, the *true* king, is mere hours away. I refuse your request for entry. You cannot expect to live a life such as yours and not reap the consequences. You will be killed, as you rightly deserve."

If Drusion knew anything about Grandfather, it was that he did not tolerate disrespect, and he would put himself into great danger just to see the insubordinate tortured.

Grandfather's hands began to shake. Drusion knew it was not magic; Grandfather had no gift for such things. No; it was clear that—for once in his long two centuries of life—he had no recourse, no allies, no way of getting what he wanted. The anger would be something terrible, Drusion knew; he would turn on whoever he could, and it was best to stay away.

Instead, he drew *Lifedrinker.* The weapon had felled many, in Grandfather's earlier years. The blade still gleamed razor-sharp. "Family." Grandfather's voice was caustic. "You have all failed me. You have brought me to ruin and I shall never forgive you. If I had half a mind I would kill you all right now. You are all worthless… every one of you."

Blame everyone but yourself, Grandfather.

"Elloré was right. You are all failures, each one of you." His sunken grey face was too monstrous to pity. "I should have listened to her. I should have killed you all, for you have only brought me low, and ruined me. Now, I miss her, after I thought I never would. She was the last capable person in our household… the last one I could trust."

Grandmother was just as wicked as you. The time seemed apt to voice the thought, but Drusion trusted his relatives as much as Grandfather. *Perhaps I trust Indryas.*

"You have brought me to ruin. Narsoli was a pious do-gooder and I am glad I killed him. He begat a fool, a vagabond, and a slut."

"Hey!" Ari bared her fangs.

"Sarsoli, you are fat and dumb."

Uncle Shakes made no response; he didn't understand much.

"Your children are both simpletons, wastes of breath. You are *all* wastes of breath, and you have ruined me. I should not have killed Elloré. I should have left her alive and killed the lot of you. You have only weighed me down. You are all weaklings."

"And you are worthless!" Ari shouted. "You are responsible for everything. Own up to it, Grandfather! It's you that's brought us down."

For a moment, Grandfather was too stunned to say anything. His eyes bulged, first in shock but then in anger. He let out a wild howl and brought his sword above him, then brought it crashing down. The point cut through Ari's tight leather, but soon the girl was gone into the veil of snow, fleeing north.

May the Dark One guide her. Though Grandfather was feeble, it was best not to voice the thought.

He had collapsed already, into the ankle-high snow. He was weeping. The sunlight was trickling away; shadow was falling upon the Great White North, and Grandfather was weeping. Drusion never thought it would happen. He wondered if his tears were acid.

Drusion had drawn out his shortsword without realizing it. He knew why, of course, but he hesitated. *What could I gain from killing Grandfather?* Sometimes it was so hard to swallow your anger and use your mind. But it felt necessary. It felt like he should do this.

A trumpet pealed from the south. The dusk was fading to night, but a yellow glow appeared far down the road. The brilliant radiance of the lightbearers could mean only one thing: the army of the Lamen Elves was coming hard and fast.

Grandfather's weeping reached a pinnacle. Drusion looked at Indryas. His brown-haired brother was stiff and immobile. Then Drusion looked back toward the approaching army, and heard the building thunder of horses' hooves. He gulped, and then took off running.

CHAPTER THREE

Indryas, son of Narsoli and Admé

One by one his relatives began to ride off. *What will they find?* Go north, east, and west, and you would find nothing. This was the end of the world, and beyond was only death. Soon Indryas found himself alone with Grandfather. He drew his own weapon, a longknife, and prepared to face the coming horde. The Lamen Elves were said to be merciful. That was their weakness, Grandfather said, and indeed, it had cost them many battles in the Great War.

"Grandfather," Indryas said. "Grandfather… they're coming."

"Indryas, the most worthless of my seed." Grandfather's voice was as biting as ever, with no trace of weeping. "Once I had gotten inside the Dundari, I was going to drink you dry, and make an example of you. I have hated you above all others. What a tragic irony, that you are the one who remains by my side."

"I have always… loved you… Grandfather." He wondered if it were true.

"And that," Grandfather said, "is why I hate you so very much." The elven prince rose, and his eyes showed no sign of tears. With *Lifedrinker* in his hands, he stood and waited for the coming storm.

~

The army stopped several yards before them. On the front lines were the Stag Riders of Non, holding lances as they sat astride the giant reindeer, their faces covered in giant horned helmets. Beyond lay many more, but the two elves in front caught Indryas' eye. One, a woman, had long brown hair and bright blue eyes. The dagged sleeves of her spidersilk robe nearly touched the ground, even on a horse. In her right hand was a staff, affixed with a bright star-gem. A lightbearer, she was; the sorceress they had heard about.

Beside her rode an elven man with long blond hair, dressed in a chain shirt. He wielded a sword and shield. "Gilden!" he shouted. "I have not come to capture you, or bring you in chains. The order of King Danirias is to bring back your head, though—now that I see it—I fear the city of Danarion will not want it anywhere within sight."

A stag rider chuckled. Indryas ground his teeth together.

"Calm yourself, Lamadon." The sorceress's voice was silken smooth. "I fear he is correct. Gilden, I can say with certainty that you deserve death. You can make this easy on yourself, or you can make it hard. It's up to you."

"If you expect me to go peacefully," Grandfather hissed, "then you are one stupid wench."

Lamadon gasped. "You *dare* speak to a lady in that manner?"

"Forbearance, Lamadon," the sorceress said with remarkable calm.

The elven warrior drew his sword. It was of *estirion,* starmetal, like Grandfather's blade—that much was clear—but instead of *Lifedrinker*'s blackish metal, it shone with a faint but perceptible yellow light. Instead of *Lifedrinker*'s skull crossguard, Lamadon's blade had a sun.

"I will call your woman a wench," Grandfather said through gritted teeth, "or a fool, or a whore, if I want to."

Lamadon's cheeks went pink. "That is the last I will hear. I must defend your honor, Your Ladyship." He galloped at Grandfather, and Indryas backed away. "The Sunblade has cut demons, and you are *nothing* compared to them!"

"Lamadon!" The sorceress' thunderous voice failed to draw him back.

The two swords kissed, and kissed again. In the midst of the fight, while Indryas was backing away, Grandfather thrust *Lifedrinker* through an opening in the horse's barding. The beast gave out a desperate screech and fell over; soldiers gasped, the horse collapsed, and Lamadon fell.

Grandfather was smiling, and his yellow smiles were terrible to behold. Lamadon stumbled as Grandfather pressed him hard.

He is going to die. Grandfather is going to win. Indryas was neither happy nor sad.

But soon enough, Grandfather landed a heavy blow, and Sunblade went spinning into the snow. Another half-second, another pause, and the *Lifedrinker* would slay Lamadon. The warrior's eyes bulged; the black starmetal sword thrust forward; and a blast of searing, heatless flame opened a hole in Grandfather's chest.

Indryas shuddered. The sorceress was riding up to them. Grandfather collapsed dead.

"My lady," Lamadon said. "You have saved me again."

Indryas stood still. *I should run.* But there was nothing to the north or east or south, only ice and death.

He and the sorceress exchanged glances. Her blue eyes held neither joy nor remorse over Grandfather's death, only calm. A silver circlet crowned her long brown hair, and her lips pressed together firmly.

Indryas had never seen a lightbearer work such magic. She had to be the most powerful of them all, a goddess among elves.

"What is your name?" she said. "Speak."

"Me?" Indryas' skin began to crawl. "I... I... my name is... erm... Lumas."

"Lies." She was smiling. "Gilden would never have his grandchild named after the Son of Light."

"Indryas," he admitted.

A sapphire pendant hanging around her neck pulsed with blue light. Indryas took a terrified step back, and realized the sorceress was beautiful.

"A strange easterly name. Mine is Amané, and I serve King Danirias." The sorceress's smile grew. "Your grandfather never showed mercy to his enemies. However, we Lamen do not kill those who ask for second chances. We will let you live if you will make an offering of atonement, say a prayer to the many faces of Light, and let the priests wash you to symbolize your repentance."

There is nothing I want less. "Of course," he said instead.

The soldiers began to murmur. A deadness had settled over Indryas.

Lamadon said, "Will we leave his foul blade here?"

The sorceress answered, "No. One of his spawn may come to get it."

As Indryas walked into the ranks of his enemies, their conversation continued:

"Will we destroy it?"

"We shall not put starmetal to waste…"

The faces of the Lamen soldiers were not condemning. They were merciful, and like Grandfather, he hated them all the more for it. *I am a monster like him, and there is nothing I want less than this.*

CHAPTER FOUR

Ari, daughter of Narsoli and Liandré

By morning, the horse was dead. The stupid sack of meat had frozen overnight, and—by the Dark One—Ari herself was cold, chilled to the bone. She'd lost track of her half-brother Drusion a while back. The sun had risen, and everything in sight was white: white drifts of snow, blinding flurries, and snow-covered hills. Even the sky looked more white than gray. *Dark One, am I cold.*

She could stand here and resign, die like some coward, but Ari wasn't a softy like Indryas or braindead like Uncle Shakes. She had a life to live, and she wasn't going to let herself die.

Dark One, is it cold. She rubbed her arms together, but that made no difference. The snow was deep. It would swallow her. Perhaps she should turn south, but she had no idea where south was.

Instead, she kept walking. It was amazing she hadn't frozen by now. The air was cold enough to freeze a fire solid, and the wind cut like a dagger into her neck. The stupid sack of meat behind her had turned into an icicle, so why hadn't she?

Perhaps, more than just bloodthirst had changed about her. At the thought of warm blood, she nearly convulsed. She needed it, more than she'd ever needed wine or food or love.

She needed blood.

~

In her wanderings throughout the following day and the next, the cold—though she hated it like hell—did not kill her. *Indeed, I've changed*, she thought more than once. *I've become more powerful, and the gods thought they were* cursing *us.*

The landscape changed little. The cold was hell, but she would never accept her fate, especially with this newfound power. Her wandering took her across lakes, frozen hard as rock, and occasional in sight of white owls and snowshoe hares. She was hungry, hungrier than she'd ever been, but she wanted blood more than food. She would give anything for a drink, to be taken to that high again, to glut herself on someone's veins. *I should feel guilty.* But she couldn't. Grandfather made sure all his offspring were immune to that weak emotion.

On the third morning, shivering uncontrollably as she stumbled through the snow, she again wondered if she should have stayed in Dundari and fought the do-gooders. Where was she going? Likely, nowhere. Ari had liked tormenting her geography tutor more than learning from him, but everyone knew that beyond Dundari—so-called Queen of the Great White North—there was nothing. Perhaps she'd get to the end of the world, and hop off.

Staggering through the biting wind and swirling drifts of snow, a thousand thoughts occurred to her: *What if I fall through the ice? What if I'm walking in circles? What if wolves are stalking me?* Then she would eye her longknife, and remember she could take care of herself.

Four days. Five days. At some point she lost count. She was starving, but couldn't move fast enough to catch the snowshoe hares, and she had no idea how to fish. She was hungry for a lot of things, but still, she wanted blood most of all.

She slept long on the sixth or seventh or thousandth night— and lay there until high noon, until the snow began to collect on her. She went on, well-rested, and continued her wandering. She realized she was going to starve. Of all the ways to die, why this?

More hours and days went by. She was in a cold, unending dream. At last she fell, starving and weak, pulled her hood tight around her ice-cold face, and resolved to never stand up again.

~

A face greeted her in the morning's light. His skin was dusky, and he was missing an eye; the other had a pale almond color. His lips were thin, and a white scar ran across his cheek. He was a human, Ari realized.

Why is there a human this far north?

Where was she?

At once he began to yap some foreign tongue. Slowly Ari rose, weak and dizzy with hunger. She eyed the man, seeing a curved knife in his hand, crusted-over with dry blood. All around him was whiteness. He was alone, Ari realized. She summoned the little strength she had left.

The man struck with a knife, but Ari glided out of the way, stepping inward, and then laid her fangs deep into his neck. The high was more intoxicating than she ever remembered. The blood warmed her better than any fire ever could. Her body sang with ecstasy. Her hunger vanished, and she continued drinking in total bliss until the human's knees gave out and he fell limp, bloodless and white as the snow that surrounded him.

Where am I, indeed? All her strength had returned; all coldness left her. Had she gone north or south, east or west? It was clear that people lived here... humans, of all creatures. If she found where they lived, she'd find food. She had killed one of their own, but if she left quickly they would never find out. She glanced at his tracks to get a good idea of where to go, and then resumed her journey. Though the blood had staved off the pain of hunger and given her strength back, she still needed food... just a little bit would be enough.

Up above, the blue skies were giving way to a dark cloud. The silence smelled of a coming storm. Around her was only white; but after she continued a while, a green horizon appeared. At the sight, she took off at a sprint. Fueled by her blood-meal, she didn't let up until the horizon took shape.

Before her lay a forest of pines. In the distance, rocky hills sometimes rose above the dark green trees. She didn't like the look of the place. She didn't like the trees or the quietness or the emptiness. For a second, she wanted nothing more than to go home. *Things would have been so much better if I'd had a different grandfather.* But she couldn't change that, now.

Seeing that human, drinking him dry, brought Ari's loneliness to the fore. She should have stayed with Drusion, her half-brother, and gone with him to wherever he chose. Should have, would have, could have. There was no point to regretting anything. She had made the decisions already. She had erred, and now she lived with the consequences.

As she gazed at the green sea around her, into the shady pines and the frozen river that snaked through them, she bit her lip. It was all she could do not to cry.

CHAPTER FIVE

Indryas, son of Narsoli and Admé

The third time the priest dunked his head in the water, Indryas reached for his longknife but found the sheath empty. *The Lamen aren't as stupid as Grandfather said.*

"O Radiant Light, purge the shadows from the soul of the lost one," the priest said for the third time. "Shine on the lost one's evil deeds, expose them, and banish them."

Indryas stood up and managed not to shout. "The gods and the light, or whatever you call it, are all well and good! But I cannot handle this." Dressed then in the orange-and-red robes of a penitent, he stormed out of the tent, wet-haired but simmering inside. Days had passed since Grandfather's death, but the tents were still pitched outside Dundari. The sorceress wouldn't let him bathe in the hot springs. In truth, he wanted to run. Perhaps he would, tonight. But beyond the snowy borderlands, there was nothing except starvation and dead cold.

Indryas stopped on the edge of camp and stared at Dundari's yellow walls. The winter solstice was coming—a time of celebration—and Indryas had to suffer through, well, *this.* He had said he was sorry, so why did he have to go through all this? His Grandfather was a wicked man, and the sorceress wasn't wrong to kill him. But why did Indryas have to suffer for it? If he had to suffer through another head-washing, he might kill somebody.

"Child." The sorceress was behind him. Indryas rolled his eyes. "Are you unwell?" she continued.

He turned around. The sorceress's sapphire pendant around her neck swelled and contracted at random; her eyes were the same color. "I... I am..." *I've lied enough.* "I am not well, not at all. I said I was sorry. I don't know why you can't accept that, and send me back to Marlon."

"Marlon?" Her laugh was joyless. "Everyone in Marlon is dead. You and your family massacred the citizens. Why would you go back there?"

"I murdered no one," Indryas growled, fuming. "I didn't drink a drop of blood."

He saw disbelief in the sorceress's blue eyes. "You are coming back to the City of Light under the protection of the King. The master healers will do their best to heal your affliction. Until you are totally cured, you will be overseen by the King's Guard."

"And if I refuse?"

She smiled derisively, like Indryas was an insolent child. "You don't have much choice, do you? You have one option before you, my friend: you must come with me, repent of your misdeeds, and enter into the City of Light. I assure you, my friend, that if there is a way to cure your affliction, the master healers will find it. Then you can walk forever in the path of Light."

There was nothing Indryas wanted less. Grandfather was a horrid man, but all this piety and religious talk was driving him mad. He needed to find his longknife; then, he needed find a horse, and flee.

He spent an hour wandering the camp grounds, peeking through whatever unguarded tents he could find. But in the end, he realized he would never find his longknife: a masterwork of steel, with a gilded skull pommel and a black hilt of eelskin and spidersilk. It had been a solstice gift from Father, long before he died, long before the Great War had broken out in earnest and things had come apart for their family. Father said he took it from a Lamen warrior after a battle, before the Years of Trial, in one of the—in hindsight—insignificant wars after Grandfather declared his independence from the King. Grandfather's smith had re-worked the sun pommel into a skull. Father said it was worth more than a country manor, though Indryas wasn't sure.

Gods, did he miss Father.

But eventually, he gave up the search. The longknife was gone, the only reminder of the life he'd lost, the last memory of Father's loving care, the only one in the family Indryas had ever trusted.

Though the longknife had vanished, horses abounded. The

Lamen cherished their horses and rode bareback whenever feasible. Huge, muscular destriers—roan and black and silver—were tied to posts or trees. But as Indryas wandered the camp grounds, looking everywhere, he eventually found what he was looking for: a horse with a saddle, wandering freely. She was not quite the size of the others, though by most measurements she'd be called a destrier.

Indryas knew it would be wiser to wait until night, but he knew the priests were waiting for him. Even now, their voices rose above the wind and the soldiers' mutters; they were singing a hymn.

"To the Light who is Lord of all the land / Whose brilliance shines through countless faces / We sing unto th—"

Indryas screamed. He hated Grandfather, and he hated the Dark One, but he hated these priests even more. He ran up to the idle horse, put a foot into a stirrup, and launched himself into the saddle. He slammed his boots into her sides hard and clucked, then took off south at a gallop.

"Horse-thief!" one of the Lamen shouted.

"The druen is escaping!" another cried.

Druen, they call us... a 'person of the night.' The name fit well, though Indryas couldn't afford to care about such things. Now, his life or death depended on the next few moments. He coaxed harder and harder, kicking and clucking and doing whatever he could to urge the horse on. She reached her uttermost gallop; then a voiced called out—*"Stop!"*—and the horse reared up, sending Indryas to the ground hard.

The air left him. His ribs shuddered, perhaps broke. He couldn't breathe. The sorceress' blue eyes soon appeared above him, and her blue sapphire pendant, waxing and waning. "Child," she said and frowned. "I have given you mercy. Why will you throw it away?"

"I am not your child!" Indryas hissed. He stood up and his ribs flared in pain as he did. He started running south. If these bewitched horses wouldn't carry him where he wanted to go, his feet would.

"I said you had one choice before you. You have spurned it!" Her voice echoed across the snow-dusted landscape. Soon the trees would hide him. "Come back, child! You only have a few moments to save yourself."

Soon the trees would hide him. The forest eaves were near. "I am not your child!" Indryas screamed.

A blast of light, soundless and heatless, flared out in front of him, like it had come from his body. When he looked down, his legs were already stumbling. *Not from my body, through it.* The sorceress had opened a hole through him, as she'd done with Grandfather. He hit the snow. "I am not your child," he would have said, but Indryas was already dead.

CHAPTER SIX

Ari, daughter of Narsoli and Liandré

After staring at the green woods before her for a long time, Ari decided to turn back. There was something about that forest she did not trust. There was something unsettling about it, something odd and old and troubling. She had nowhere to go, but given the choice, she would go nowhere. She turned back and walked again into the endless white. Snow was beginning to fall heavily, now. She had not taken ten steps before strangers surrounded her.

They had the same dusky complexion and brown eyes of the human Ari had drunken dry. Fur lined their heavy robes. All of them, men and women both, held spears. Ari's gut clenched, and it dawned on her that she would not survive if they came to blows. She stopped herself from touching her longknife.

"Hello," she said.

One of them spoke: a young man of less than twenty, dark eyes and black hair, and a broken nose. A few of the others yapped in return, but in their case, they were not looking at Ari.

She couldn't breathe. She could not understand a word in their language. The young man took her by the hand, and Ari thought better of resisting. She followed the humans down into a valley, where the forests began.

~

A collection of hide tents overlooked a frozen lake. The young man worked at starting a fire, while his tribe wandered off, doing whatever needed doing. Fishing, Ari thought. Hunting, perhaps. The fear in the pit of Ari's stomach grew with each passing hour.

In time, they came back with hunks of meat. Many were covered in blood; they were off butchering an animal, Ari realized. In time, the young man had started a fire, and his fellow tribesmen stuck bits of meat onto skewers. But Ari did not want to eat.

Through the night she understood nothing. An old man, late middle-aged, gave Ari the most unnerving looks as he sat across from her. The fire lighted in his eyes, and he looked more demon than man.

Ari refused the food, but the tribesmen did not take offense; in fact, they seemed glad. The sun had gone away for several hours, and Ari was nodding off to sleep; then the young man woke her, and took her by the hand. He led her into a tent, and motioned her to lay on the fur floor. Then, he began to undress.

If I resist, they will kill me. I cannot struggle. Still, tears welled in her eyes. They had called her "the loosest wench in Marlon," so why was she crying? The tears did not stop him. In time they were one.

~

In the cold of the morning, she was back on her feet, though sore. Her lover—or captor—was donning his hooded fur cloak. She walked outside, feeling weak and vulnerable. The cold hit her like the blow of a cudgel. Her foot was unsure as she walked into the snow, and she half-slipped.

The man from last night was waiting for her. He had a spear in hand, and meant to use it. She could read it in his coals of eyes that he meant to kill her. She stepped back, stumbled again, and fell. Her hand hit the powdery snow. She began to tremble. At the same time, her captor emerged from the tent and began screaming at him, at her would-be assailant. He backed down and lowered his spear. At some point, she discerned her captor's name from the yapping: Kaneet.

Kaneet. And there, Ari was. With Kaneet, at the edge of the world where no one could find her. There was food, but there was certain death.

She began to weep all over again, and by morning's end her tears were frozen.

CHAPTER SEVEN

Drusion, son of Narsoli and Admé

What began as a group of twelve had dwindled to three. Though, after endless days of journeying, they'd reached the sea, the wolves in the north hunted sentient beings selectively. Even now, in a world of green forests and thinly-frozen lakes, the wolves seemed to disregard the reindeer and hares, and hunt the elves above all. The only way to distract them was by running when they caught one. They'd torn Gomé and Gildion's throats and devoured them as Drusion and his ragtag band went running.

Now that most his nieces and nephews were eaten, Drusion had the worst of company: Uncle Shakes, waste of breath that he was, and his two halfwit spawn, Sarsi and Sarsé. With each passing day, Drusion grew to hate them more.

At times, he'd burst out laughing at the hopelessness of the situation. There were no walled towns to protect them from the wolves. Inevitably, they'd face the beasts' fangs and lose. They were, simply put, doomed.

The days and weeks blended together, but at some point, they had begun following a river. Through its twists and turns, they had no shortage of thorns and thickets, or discouraging blasts of freezing wind. But as dusk fell one evening and a wolf's howl heralded their certain doom, the frozen river led them to an unfrozen sea.

Drusion had never been to the Eastern Sea, but here it was. This had to be one of the northernmost bounds of it, but it was a sea.

And he grew weak and faint at what met his eyes next: a walled town with open gates. He had half a thought of asking them to shut it, and let Sarsi, Sarsé and their halfwit father die, but that was too much effort for the moment. Instead, he ran.

There, among the buildings of this impossibly northern town, he collapsed and realized how hungry he was. Hungry for food... and other things.

~

The people of the town were elves, and mostly males. When they spoke, they did so in the southern dialect.

"Who are you?" said one, a man with long black hair, stern grey eyes, and a light shirt of chainmail.

"Drusion," he muttered. "Drusion…"

For a while, there was no response. "What has happened to you? How has the son of the Dark Prince fallen so far from fortune?"

A familiar desperation overtook him. He could not tell the truth, not the whole truth at least. "The King of the Elves drove us from Marlon… he chased us to Dundari, and I ran all the way here."

"And why would our town want to aid an enemy of the King?"

Drusion looked up and despaired at the unforgiving grey eyes. "Because it is the right thing…"

"You want us to do the right thing, just as Prince Gilden always did."

The irony was not lost on him. "No… Just because it's right." But perhaps it wasn't even that.

"One moment," the elf said, turned, and walked away.

A few minutes later, another man stood before him. This one was lanky, probably half again Drusion's height. His arms were long and thin, but muscular. A curved saber hung from his belt. He had no left hand.

In an instant, it dawned on him.

"Drusion, son of the Dark Prince, begs for his life in front of his father's enemy, Noresti Andomas."

Drusion slowly stood up. "King" Andomas had been a thorn in Grandfather's side during the Great War. He had been one of Grandfather's subjects, a mercenary from the Riverlands on the edge of the Eastern Sea. When Grandfather sided with the Dark One, Andomas led a widespread rebellion. Halfway through the war, Grandfather won a costly victory over him and left Andomas with a decisive wound: a severed left hand. He retreated with a small fleet, but a storm drowned them. Or so Grandfather said.

Andomas was smiling. "Ah, it is truly poetic justice. My enemy's own son begs for his life, swears fealty to me. Honor says I should not leave you alive."

Drusion was shaking, now. "My lord Andomas, I have found the Light. I have found the countless faces from where it shines. I have changed. I am not my grandfather." He was lying through his teeth.

"Spare me." Andomas chuckled. "Trust me: I did not oppose your father for that reason, Drusion. Your false conversion is doing you no favors." The smile on his face grew. "There is no god, nor are there gods. There is only Nothing; and may all elves know this and revere Her name."

He should have known. Andomas was like his fellow southerners. The Lonen tribe's religious beliefs had been the cause of many wars. He looked back. Sarsi, Sarsé, and Uncle Shakes were right behind him. The gates were open, and a howl echoed from the woods. The wolves were coming.

"The wolves of the far north love elven flesh better than does or stags." Andomas' smile seemed more wicked than jovial, now. "Give me one reason why I shouldn't let them eat you. You are the son of my enemy. I never forgive. I never forget."

"All the wealth of Marlon could be yours. Grandfather retook it, and he will pay dearly for our safe return."

"Grandfather is dead!" bellowed Sarsé.

Drusion looked back and snarled. That chubby, cross-eyed halfwit would be the end of him. He wanted to kill her right then, right there.

Andomas was laughing, now. "Ah, Drusion, what a pity you have such siblings. They have cost you your life. The wolves of the north are big as bulls. You won't stand a chance against them."

Drusion looked back again, muscles tense and hard as stone. Out of the black pines, large furry shapes were emerging.

But the gates were closing; one of Andomas' men was cranking a wheel, and the doors were going to shut. "I hold grudges," Andomas said, "but I am not a fool. I opposed your Grandfather because he was a fool. He acted out of malice. If the Dark One had deposed the gods and won the war, would that have been good for any of us? Would the Dark One have remembered your grandfather, Drusion, or would he have consigned Gilden to the flame like everyone else?"

"I thought you did not believe in the gods."

"When you see what happened in the Great War, it's difficult to deny that there is more than Nothing. Some of my people clung to their belief in the Black Lady, and I admire their faith; but I did not. Regardless of whether the westerners are right, I saw a demon destroy swaths of the Riverlands, and I did not want that. Regardless, Drusion, I did not lie. I do not care about god or the gods or the Light. I saw your Grandfather, and I saw what he had done, and I did not like it."

Drusion looked back at the shut gates. "You are a complex man, Andomas. Why have you left me alive?"

"I assure you that mercy has nothing to do with it." Andomas smiled again. "The king and queen of Londor are aware of my city and my presence. They call my settlement Port Andom, and have requested that I explore the waters of the North Sea."

"So they have seceded from Grandfather's kingdom."

"Grandfather is dead," Sarsé said.

Drusion glared at her and snarled, "Shut up!" It was all he could do not to kill her.

When he looked back, Andomas was smiling. "To answer your question, Drusion, the king and queen announced their independence weeks ago. Long enough for word to travel this far north. And to answer your other question, Drusion, on why you have been left alive... you won't like this, I'm afraid. The King and Queen of Londor have officially sanctioned the selling of slaves."

"Grandfather always has."

"Yes, but in Naremon and East Arlom and the Riverlands, it never was," Andomas said. "Now, my dear friend, His Majesty King Aimon will pay dearly to see Gilden's offspring humiliated under the yoke of slavery. For the lot of you, I am sure he will pay at least fifty Yan... enough to build a temple to the Black Lady, or a wondrous dock for ships. Fifty gold pieces alive, he said, or twenty dead. You'll be placed in prison a good while before we have a proper ship to transport you. It will be a long journey to Naremon, but I'm afraid—in time—you will wish you'd been eaten by wolves."

CHAPTER EIGHT

Ari, daughter of Narsoli and Liandré

A day, then a week, then a month. With each passing moment, Ari's dread grew. Kaneet, her captor and lover, protected her—that much was clear—but she never felt safe. Little by little she began to understand their language, and when she and Kaneet had their first full conversation, her dire situation dawned on her.

"We are the first men," Kaneet told her. "We were here when the world was young. Once, food was plenty. Now it's hard to find fish, hard to find berries and edible food. We eat bark when we're hungry. The other tribes of the first men are not so moral. They serve Mugluk, the Bringer of Winter. His children are the Half-Men, and the other tribes beyond our camp."

Even now, Ari could not love him. He protected her and he was the only reason she lived, but she felt nothing for him. She wanted her brothers and sisters, and the life she'd always known. "When you say... they are not so moral..." She still struggled to speak the language, though she understood it well. "What do you mean?"

"Mugluk tempts us to eat the meat of men."

She felt like vomiting.

"The chieftain knows you killed Pakak."

She remembered the man she'd drunk dry. His blood had warmed her better than any fire ever could.

"He does not care because Pakak gave in to Mugluk. He was starving like the rest of us, but he gave in to the Bringer of Winter and ate man-flesh. He would have killed you and eaten your meat, but you killed him. Chieftain was happy."

I need to get out of here, she realized. *I need to run...*

"Mugluk whispers in men's minds... Mugluk tells men to eat their own. But once you've eaten man's meat there is no going back. You turn into Mugluk's servant. You turn into a cannibal. The other tribes serve Mugluk, now. All except us."

She remembered the pot of meat they cooked the night she came. The meat she didn't eat. She wondered. Was it Pakak? At the thought, she retched. "Will you take me away from here?" she asked. "I need to find my family."

"The White Waste surrounds us," Kaneet said. "There is no food."

"There is no food here, either."

Kaneet smiled for the first time ever; but it was a faint, sad smile. "The White Waste is full of Half-Men, servants of Mugluk."

"Half-Men," Ari breathed, but she meant it as a question.

Kaneet did not disappoint. "We call them Half-Men because they look like giant men... they have two feet, two arms, a head and a nose and eyes. But they are Half-Men because they are not like us. They don't talk. They don't wear clothes. They don't think, they only eat. They are more like bears or wolves than men. They are the children of Mugluk."

A hot tear dripped down Ari's eye. Kaneet wiped it away.

"But there is a legend... our shaman Tuktu used to tell the tale. He said there is a place beyond the White Waste, a land of plenty where there are animals and berries and fish. He said he went there... He told me how to get there. That was before he gave into Mugluk and ate Chieftain's son."

"Will you take me there?" Ari said.

"No." Kaneet's face was somber. He stood to his feet, and left.

Winter was descending upon them. When Ari told Kaneet she didn't want to leave the tent, the tribesmen did not argue. She remained inside as an arctic chill settled into the valley. A shivering spread over her like an illness. If the cold claimed her, perhaps it would be a mercy, but even now she didn't want to die. She had a life to live, even now. The thought of death still terrified her. *Am I shaking because it's cold, or because I'm afraid?*

Above the wind and the crackling fire, the tribesmen were talking in low tones. Eventually, she made them out: "She is not one of the first men. She is not one of us. She may be a child of Mugluk. If we eat her, we won't be transgressing..."

"Shut up, Tartuk!" Kaneet sounded angry. "She is one of the first men. I can tell."

"I am not sure," said a woman's voice.

Kaneet snarled something Ari didn't understand. "How quickly do you give in to Mugluk. She is one of the first men—I know it! She has not eaten man's flesh. She will stay alive!"

"Did she eat Pakak?"

"We all did. Pakak was given up to Mugluk. According to our law, we—"

As I thought. The meat was human.

"You have fallen for this girl, Kaneet." The chieftain's voice was low but loud. "Your love is blinding your judgment. The girl is not one of the first men. She wandered into the valley from the White Waste. We are all hungry. Our babies cry for food. We may not survive the winter. If she is not one of the first men, it will not be a transgression; nor will it be a surrender to Mugluk. She is a gift, Kaneet... a gift of food from our ancestors."

"No!" Kaneet hissed. "I won't let you take her. I won't let you have her. She is a first man. She is—"

"*Silence!*" Ari never heard the chieftain angry, but it was a terrifying thing. "Your judgment is clouded by Mugluk. It is clear that she is a gift from beyond. Women, ready your spices. Tomorrow night, we feast."

A few of them cheered. Ari's shivering became shaking. Kaneet entered the tent. He had changed. He looked sad. No, afraid. "Ari, I have changed my mind. When everyone is asleep, we will go. We will enter the White Waste together, and go to the land of plenty."

CHAPTER NINE

Sarsi, son of Sarsoli and Elloré

The prison was dark and wet, but the food was worse. Sarsi cared nothing for the gods, nor the faces of Light, nor heaven, but Grandfather had done this to himself. He had done this to all of them. If he had just left Grandmother alone, none of this would have happened. At least, that's what Lorlé had said. It was a curse from the gods, she said. All because Grandfather killed Grandmother... though he'd done a lot worse.

The slop that Andomas gave them wasn't fitting for a hog, much less the grandson of a prince. Sarsi wondered if he made it terrible on purpose. Dark One knows, his cooks put no effort into it. It was a ground-up mash of everything they didn't like, with some saltwater added. Cousin Drusion wouldn't even touch it. Cousin Drusion was too dignified. Sister, however, was shoveling it down like it was one of Grandfather's feasts. Sarsi supposed she couldn't tell the difference.

Father was the same. Sarsi knew that Father was a halfwit like everybody said, and so was Sister, so what did that say about him? Grandmother said their mother was a slave the family captured in the war, and he supposed he got his full wits from the mother he never knew. As he sat there, watching Father shovel down the slop like a hog, he grimaced in shame. He was damned thirsty for blood, but he knew better than to attack one of Andomas' men. A lot of them had big head cleavers of swords—bastard swords, they called them in the south-country—and others had bows for killing at a long range. They were as good as stuck here, for now.

Andomas said a ship was coming to take them down southways, and they'd be slaves for the rest of their lives. One time Sarsi had gone far away with Grandfather to the Riverlands. It was before the Great War broke out. Grandfather hadn't been as cruel back then. He didn't even kill anyone during the trip, except for a few slaves.

It was a tour, he had told Sarsi, and he wanted him to be there. He said he'd rather Drusion have come with him, but Drusion had been with the King.

Sarsi didn't want to go back to the Riverlands. The elves of the Riverlands worshiped the Black Lady instead of the gods, which he would ordinarily like. But that goddess would have no problems with the River-folk beating Sarsi or torturing him. The River-folk wouldn't treat Sarsi kindly, because he had Grandfather's blood in him.

A door opened and slammed shut. The gaoler, Narrias, came walking in. He was bigger than Andom, but he was also clumsier. He had a bastard sword with a huge blade, but Drusion said he was slow, and probably a halfwit. Sarsi looked at Father, who was now licking his bowl like some dog. The biggest halfwit in the room was behind bars.

"I will take your bowls," Narrias grunted. "Andomas said he wants get your slime scrubbed off them."

He opened the door, and Father's bowl hit the floor with a clatter. Father looked up at Narrias. The glint in his eyes indicated he was about to do something stupid.

Up Father got, flying to his feet. Narrias reached for his bastard sword but Father had already sunk his teeth into the lout's white neck. Father was guzzling his blood. Soon, sister joined him.

Sarsi whimpered and stood up, trembling all over. Narrias weakened more and more as the seconds went by. The half-minute seemed an hour, but soon the gaoler had gone white and bloodless, limp as a sack.

Father and Sister ran out of the cell. Sarsi took off after them, not knowing what else to do. They ran toward the door. He glanced over his shoulder, and Drusion was not behind him.

The air outside hit him like a wall, far colder than the drafty cell. A freezing maelstrom of wind bit him like daggers from all sides. Thick white flurries obscured their vision. Father was running, grunting like an animal, and Sister was following him. They were running for the gate. Sarsi sprinted after them.

"Hey! Look!" a voice called out, above the howling wind. A

few of Andomas' men were running for Father.

Halfwit, slob, or degenerate, Father was still Father. As one of them came charging with a bastard sword ready to cleave, Sarsi charged as fast as he could. He hit the assailant before the sword could take Father, bowling him over onto the snow-packed ground. The bastard sword skidded from his hands, and Sarsi made a leap for it, grasping the hilt as more of Andomas' men appeared out of the doors of the houses.

Dark One, is it heavy. Father had disappeared through the veil of snow. The gate was cranking shut. Father had abandoned him, left him here to die. *I shouldn't be surprised, but I am.*

Out of the freezing arctic wind and whirling snow, the tall lithe shape of Andomas appeared. In the gray light, the curved saber seemed wickedly sharp. The mercenary—longtime thorn in Grandfather's side—was smiling. "Ah, you've erred gravely. We will find your pig father and pig sister in time. They'll be punished. But you, pig-spawn—I've forgotten your name—"

"Sarsi..."

"—you have not gotten as far as them. Sending you south as a corpse will set me back a few Yan, but it's better than risking your escape."

"I... No. No!" Sarsi was going rigid. "I'll do anything, Andomas. Anything you wish, I'll do. Anything at all..."

Andomas charged him and struck hard with the curved saber. Sarsi brought the bastard sword up weakly, just barely parrying the first strike; but it threw him off for the second, which came hard and fast from the other side. The blade bit through his neck, and he went flying, or so it seemed, but it was his head that went flying, and an instant after he realized that, he was dead.

CHAPTER TEN

Drusion, son of Narsoli and Admé

When Andomas came to the gaol once again, he was holding Sarsi's head by its sparse black hair. "Your cousin. He tried to escape." He dropped it, and the head hit the floor with a squishing sound.

Drusion felt nothing. He did not care one way the other about Uncle Shakes or his halfwit spawn. "I am sorry to see it," he lied.

Andomas smiled. "You have acted the wiser. Your uncle and your other cousin ran off. They will be found soon."

Again, Drusion felt nothing, and this time he said nothing.

"Stay put, and you will be taken care of. Your uncle and your cousin will regret their decision gravely."

"Regret is beyond them," Drusion said. "They are both simple-minded."

Andomas smiled. It looked like he wanted to say something, but instead—after a pause—he turned and left for the door. The gaoler scowled at him.

~

A week later, Andomas returned. "A ship has arrived."

In the mercenary's grey eyes, Drusion glimpsed something more beyond his words.

"It is a strong oceangoing vessel, the best of its kind. Pray you don't get seasick on the long journey south."

"I don't pray," Drusion said.

Andomas smiled. "A true son of Gilden."

"*Grandson.*"

"It is all right." Andomas grinned. "I do not pray either."

~

The oceangoing vessel, a large cog, docked in the harbor. It had a black sail with red accents: the symbol of Londor and her king and queen. Drusion approached it as slowly as he could. *A lifetime of slavery... perhaps death would be preferable.* But in truth, he'd rather live.

He climbed aboard the cog and gazed around the deck. The first face he saw was Drassané, his cousin, and her toddling children Hagon and Gilthasi. In the distance was Druthor, brother of Drassané, and his daughters Sildané and Bensané.

A captain, a man of Londor by the looks at him and no relative of Drusion's, was piloting the ship. He was taking them all as slaves to the south-lands, Drusion guessed, until he looked back and saw his cousin Dralynthi down in the port, handing Andomas a pouch that was doubtlessly full of gold.

"We took all the gold we could from Grandfather's vault." Drusion looked back Drassané. A smile had spread across her white moon-like face. "It took a lot of effort to convince Dralynthi. Never say I don't care about you, cousin."

Drusion laughed. He and his cousin had been bedfellows once. He had professed his love for her, yes. But even now—saved by this woman that loved him—he realized he wouldn't have done the same for her.

CHAPTER ELEVEN

Ari, daughter of Narsoli and Liandré

"Do you know where we are?" Ari said.

"Of course," Kaneet said, but his voice trembled and she knew beyond a doubt that the truth was no.

The White Waste, as the "first men" called it, stretched around them into the horizon. The drifts of snow reached her breasts, and, in some places, above her head. Wherever there wasn't blinding whiteness, huge formations of ice and hardened snow towered above them like abstract sculptures. The flurries blinded Ari, swirling around and obscuring all vision, and the air was so cold that every breath burned her throat. Even in her thick, fur-lined cloak, she shivered. What a mistake she'd made.

I threw my life away when I ran from Grandfather. She wanted to cry but she'd cried all her tears away already. Crying was her last comfort, her last way to expel the feeling of doom, but even that had been taken from her.

And something was hunting them.

Kaneet did his best to assure her that nothing was hunting them. But she saw the look in his eyes when the roar echoed across the White Waste. It wasn't the roar of a bear, Ari knew, though Kaneet said that there were, in fact, bears this far north. No, this roar sounded more like a yell than a roar; more human or elven than ursine, like a strained yet impossibly loud scream. Every time it happened, Kaneet stumbled, or so it seemed to Ari. *He is weak, too. He is not immune to fear.*

Did she love him? She didn't know. He certainly loved her, and that endeared him to her more than anything else. Grandfather had said Ari spread her legs for half of Marlon—an untrue insult, though she had more experience than most, and much more than Kaneet. In fact, sometimes it felt like he didn't know what he was doing, and it had not surprised her a bit when Kaneet said she was his first.

The days were short and it seemed they were growing shorter. The sun was already setting, though it seemed like it had just risen. The sky was losing its color, and soon darkness would set in. They were passing through a depression in the snow, a road of ice, when Kaneet stumbled and fell. "I'm hungry," he merely said.

In an instant, she had tears again, dripping down her cheeks. She was weak, and hungry, too. She couldn't go on without food. She couldn't keep walking. Kaneet didn't know where he was going. They were here, trapped in the White Waste, and completely alone. He had no idea how to get to the land of plenty, and it had probably been the pipe-dream of some shaman. She shut her eyes and fell limp. Even breathing seemed an arduous task.

Kaneet was on top of her.

"Not now," Ari muttered. "Not now..." But he was determined to have his way. He wrapped his arms around her, went in for a kiss, and she bit and drank.

His veins filled her like the richest of feasts. His blood, as it traveled through her, warmed her like the hottest of summers. The red liquor took her mind higher than any wine or bedding ever had. And too soon it was over. Kaneet lay atop her, limp; and her only friend in the whole world, the only one who had a chance of saving her, was dead.

The roar that came then—echoing over the snow and ice—sent her scrambling to her feet. She had no time for guilt or mourning, though she knew she should feel both. As the sky darkened to purple overhead, she ran and didn't look back.

The sun was just a twinkling in the horizon when the scream echoed once more. Her muscles had turned to jelly but she couldn't afford to look back. She had to survive, she had to live, she wouldn't let herself die no matter what.

Footsteps echoed through the howling White Waste. Ice broke off, and at last Ari couldn't help but look back.

What she saw froze her for a half-second. The thing was seven, maybe eight or nine feet tall. It two legs and two arms like a man or an elf, but it was neither: its face was flat, its eyes were beady, and two yellow teeth stuck up from its lips like tusks. Shaggy brown hair covered everything except its leathery face. It let out another scream. *It's one of the Half-Men.*

She sprinted ahead, putting all her energy into it but knowing the Half-Man was faster. The sun was fading, the sky was growing dark, and Ari kept sprinting, not for Kaneet or anyone but herself. She slipped and hit the ice, then skidded across it in the snow. The Half-Man was charging at her on all fours. At last one of its leathery gray hands wrapped round Ari's waste and pressed tight. Would it swallow her now? Would it crush her like a grape?

No; it was taking her somewhere, taking her along. Would it have mercy on her? Would she survive? She would have to wait.

~

The Half-Man's den had shelter from the wind. *Count your blessings.* A do-gooder priest had told Ari that, before Grandfather burned him alive.

She might have hope if she hadn't opened her eyes. Blood stained the ice floor of the cave. Bones were piled everywhere. One set in the center looked like a recent kill: a bear, maybe. The Half-Man grunted as it sucked out the last of the marrow.

When the Half-Man's beady black eyes looked into her, and it began to grunt violently, Ari shrieked. The terror broke something free in her. She took off running, out of the cave toward the White Waste and the endless snow.

The Half-Man grabbed her before she got outside. It dragged her back into the cave. It hit her with the bone. She struggled harder, and it hit her again. She was crying now. *I won't die. I won't die. I can't. I'm too young.* She broke free for a moment but the Half-Man grabbed her again. It hit her harder than ever. It was shrieking now, half bestial and half humanoid, a wretched sound that sickened Ari even as it propelled her further on.

She struggled again to break free. The bone came down with

shattering force and she slipped unconscious. The Half-Man began to eat.

CHAPTER TWELVE

Drusion, son of Narsoli and Admé

Where had his family gone, he wondered. The cold had claimed Indryas and Ari, perhaps. Now, he was alone with his cousins on the North Sea.

They were going north. The captain—an uncursed elf by the name of Thorlongas—and his bare-bones crew, said they'd been to a land on the edge of the world, an island of life east of the White Wastes and just south of what he called the Ever-Ice. In this empty, uninhabited land, he claimed that fish and game abounded, and crops might even grow.

"A hundred Yan. Even Andomas couldn't refuse a price like that." His cousin Drassané stood behind him. They'd become bedfellows once again, though making love on a ship, with its constant rocking, was not an ideal choice. "I wonder if it was worth it."

"Of course it was." Drusion was indebted to her, now, he realized. He had no doubts his cousin would make full use of it.

The North Sea's roiling waves crashed frequently against the wood of the cog. At night, the darkness was near pitch. By day, the skies had a dark blue color and the sun rarely shone its face. The water was so cold it burned Drusion's cheeks whenever it sprayed onto the deck. It was a miracle it did not freeze over like everything else of the Far North.

They'd been at sea for how long, he wondered. He'd lost count, but he guessed it was more than a week. The provisions—a mix of god-awful salted meat and stale biscuits—worsened Drusion's seasickness. *At least I am alive*, he told himself as the cog drove through the crashing waves.

~

On the tenth day, a while after the day's light had dawned,

Thorlongas shouted that they neared land. Tiny Hagon and Gilthasi yelled out in excitement and their mother did her best to quiet them. Their journey was not over yet. There were things left to be done.

But as the horizon appeared, and the sun peeked through dark clouds, spreading silver light across the freezing sea and onto the dense forest of pines, Drusion couldn't help but feel hopeful.

~

When Drusion had two feet on the ground, he had to put a hand on a tree-trunk to stay steady. He was not a man of the sea, and standing on solid ground washed through him like an elixir. The sailor Thorlongas stood with them. The air was cold but dry.

"Is there anything else?" Thorlongas asked, "or may I depart for the Riverlands? It is a long journey."

Drassané's eyes met his. They were asking him a question: *Shall we drink?* But Drusion saw how Uncle Shakes' stupidity had gotten the best of them. His mind burned with desire to drink Thorlongas dry. But unlike Sarsoli and his children, he would think before he acted. "No," Drusion asserted. "There is nothing else at all. May you have a pleasant journey back."

Drassané's eyes revealed her disappointment, but she also knew he was right.

CHAPTER THIRTEEN

Drusion, son of Narsoli and Admé

"What shall we name our new country?"

Drassané's question seemed silly in the nascent spring. The air had warmed from a deathly freeze to a slight chill, and Dralynthi had already killed a doe. After much trial and error, and a few lessons from the scant recollections of his cousin Druthor, they had constructed a settlement of sorts a mile from the sea, hugging the banks of what they called the Black River. Three log houses suited the small family well.

Drusion, Drassané, and her two children lived together now. They hadn't bothered with the marriage ritual. They had no antipriest to officiate, and it seemed a bothersome technicality. For better or worse, they were together, and Drassané was large with child.

"What shall we name the new country?" Drusion repeated the question. "Is it even a country?"

"It will be a kingdom," Drassané said, "and you will be the king."

Drusion half-smiled. "What an imagination you have. Shall we call it Drusindur, the land of Drusion?"

"Be more modest," Drassané said with a playful grin. "What of your father, my uncle? Shall we name your kingdom after him?"

"My kingdom." Drusion laughed. "Narsoldur, after my father Narsoli."

"It doesn't flow," Drassané said. "What of Nardur?"

"Nardur, the Black Land. It fits well, and flows much easier off the tongue. Nardur it is, my queen…"

~

A horn blew. They had no horns and nothing to make them with. It could mean only one thing: intruders.

Drusion ran out the log house doors, knife in hand. Through the trees, the white-blue banners of the Lamen appeared, and the flowing red and gold robes of the do-gooder priests. A few of the Nurnen stag riders had come as well, clopping forward in their heavy armor, but their number was far fewer than in Dundari.

"On behalf of King Gilesti Danirias and by the counsel of Andomas, we have scoured the wilderness. We have finally found the rats' nest." A pudgy, bald-headed elf in red and gold robes was talking, he noticed after a few second's search. "Here they are: the druen, the vampires, the children of the night."

The name was not bad at all. Drusion smiled sadly. "Where is the witch?" he said. "Surely you wouldn't come to destroy us without her."

"Such assumptions." The pudgy elf smiled. "The *witch*, as you call her, has left our army. Amané and her new husband Lamadon have ventured south, seeking the legend of the Heavenly Orchard."

A legend that never passed into Drusion's ears. He didn't care to find out more. "She abandoned you for superstition. Not a wise woman, it seems."

"She is wiser than you will ever be." Despite the insult, the pudgy elf sounded chipper.

The door behind Drusion opened, and Drassané peeked out, then instantly ducked inside.

"And now you have come to kill us."

"Wrong," he said. "Dorias?" Another man in red-gold robes walked up and handed over a vellum scroll.

"This is an agreement between King Gilesti Danirias and you to be stored in the Great Library. It says you, nor any of your people, will leave this wilderness, nor go beyond Port Andom; and none of your people may tarry in Port Andom for more than one day and one night. In exchange, the Eternal King will leave your people unbothered, to eke out whatever existence you choose."

Drusion put his sigil on the scroll all right, but he would not keep it; he only wanted the Lamen to leave forever.

And soon they were gone.

~

That night, they had a feast to celebrate the departure of the Lamen. Dralynthi cooked up venison steaks and juicy trout, though Drusion hungered for blood most of all.

Cursed, I am, he thought as he stared across the fire into Drassané's wonderfully wicked eyes. He had no doubt they'd share a bed tonight. The King would leave them unbothered. It would give them time to gather strength and build a society out of this wild land. The blood hunger was their curse, but it was also a blessing beyond any pleasure known to elves.

He bit into the seared venison steaks, and felt the blood trickle into his mouth. It was a beginning, not an end. The vampire race would live on and the King would not harry them. The world would learn to fear the druen, the children of the night.

Drusion smiled, again peering into his cousin's black eyes. *Cursed I am*, he thought, *but blessed.*

VAMPIRE BLADE

CHAPTER ONE:
IRON WOMAN

A corrupting wind blew from the south into the northernmost reaches. In its wake, the edges of swords filmed over with rust, the ploughs of the coastland druen became useless, and the air tinged with the smell of a strange metal. When at last the wind reached the mouth of the Black River, a ship appeared in the horizon: a giant tortoise-like craft with many sails, obviously from far away. And when it reached the harbor, a woman arrived: black-haired, dark-eyed, and pale as all the druen around her. She clutched a staff in her ivory hands, and she called herself the Iron Sorceress.

~

Druthor the Great, King of the Vampires

King Druthor sat as he always did on the Crimson Throne, in the midst of the black-bricked walls of the royal castle. When a servant pushed open the great wooden doors of the throne room, interrupting him without warning, his teeth protracted and he stood up, having half a mind to drink him dry right then, right there.

"Your Worship!" he shouted. "There is an intruder. She says she comes from the southlands, from Londor! She wants to have an audience with you. She has something she wants to give you!"

"Send the Red Guard to kill her," Druthor hissed. *How dare this servant bother me?* He inched closer.

"The Red Guard tried, Your Worship. The woman bent their swords into useless clubs. It seems she has power over metal. She is a wizar—"

"*Silence!*" Druthor hissed. There were spears in the throne room. If he spoke again he'd hurl one. "I will hear her out."

The servant bobbed his head and disappeared through the throne room doors, knowing full well what danger he was in.

"Who are you?" Druthor hissed when the woman showed her face.

If her features were a trifle more predatory, her movements a trifle more catlike, she could easily pass as a druen. Blue-gray eyes stared intensely into Druthor's. Red lips stood out starkly against her bloodless face. An ash-gray robe fell to her feet, and a silver rope belt clung tight to her waste. In her hand was a staff of dark wood. "I am Liandré, Sorceress of the Iron Coven. I come from the Iron Isle, and I bring goodwill from his majesty King Aimon the Second."

"What do you want, witch?" Druthor hissed. Unprotected as he was, he knew how unwise attacking her would be. "Speak!"

"His majesty King Aimon is engaged in a war with the westerners. Danarion, the City of Light, lies unprotected. While our armies fight at the border, you have an opportunity to destroy the do-gooders once and for all. The Lamen have been your ancient foe ever since your ancestor Prince Gilden—"

"Do not talk of him," Druthor hissed. "You know nothing of him."

For a second, the Iron Sorceress looked afraid. But whatever glimmer of fear there was in her eyes quickly evaporated. "Ah, druen-king. I apologize if I spoke too rashly. You see, there is something in the City of Light you may want..."

"Lies," Druthor hissed again. "There is nothing. The only thing I want is the Lamen's blood."

"And you will get it. But you are wrong."

Druthor jerked forward and nearly pounced right then, right there.

"There is something you want. Your grandfather's blade... *Lifedrinker.* The one they stole from you. It lies in a secret vault. And I know where to get it. *Lifedrinker* is a symbol of national pride. Do you not want it, King Druthor? The druen-kings deserve the blade their ancestor wielded. It is criminal that the Lamen have it."

"Yes, yes." Druthor stood erect, and the pulsing anger left him. "I shall muster an army. Their blood will fill the streets and I... I... will hold my grandfather's blade."

"Caution," the Iron Sorceress intoned. "The army must be fleet of foot. And the White Wastes are treacherous. Cavalry is best—"

"Quiet, wench!" Druthor snapped. "You know nothing of the White Wastes. If you are coming with us you shall learn to respect the king."

"Yes, my lord. Of course."

Druthor looked into the woman's steely eyes. He took a step forward. *What use is she now*, he wondered. *She cannot help me.* Her magic-weaving would help them enter Danarion, perhaps, but in the end it was clear that her life had little use. Looking at her red lips brought bloodlust to the forefront of his mind. The King and Queen of the Vampires had—since the dawn of their nation—benefited from the Right of First Blood. Anyone who intruded into the Black Castle had as good as offered himself as a bloodmeal.

Spears would not work; their heads were metal. Nor could a sword, for obvious reasons. Clad in nothing but his bloodred royal robe, Druthor pounced at her, flying through the air and preparing to tackle her to the ground; but the Iron Sorceress somersaulted out of the way, and Druthor hit the stone floor hard.

As he stood up, heart pounding, the change in the air was palpable. An eldritch gleam danced in the iron woman's eyes. Iron flew through the air; from spearheads and tools throughout the throne room. Druthor ran at her again, but then spikes of iron were slamming into the floor, breaking up the priceless stonework. A sheet of metal fell from overhead; and Druthor was in a prison of the witch's own making, complete with impenetrable iron bars.

Liandré was cackling now. "I am the most powerful magic weaver living. And you thought you could overpower me? Oh, Druthor, you may be lord of the vampires, but you have so very much to learn."

Druthor flushed hot in embarrassment. Then he laughed—a chuckle at first—and then cackled along with the sorceress. *I erred indeed.* "I will go with you, Liandré," he said. "I will go with you to the City of Light, to reclaim my ancestor's sword. The druen respect only strength; and you have proven yourself strong."

~

Two days later, the greatest army Nardur had ever seen departed from Druenel-Hai. Five thousand soldiers in total—two-hundred Blood Knights, eight-hundred men of the Red Guard, three-thousand footsoldiers, a few hundred crossbowmen and a few dozen Black Zealots. The vampire lords rarely worked together, but their king Druthor had ordered a muster of everything they had. With them followed a train of slaves, a thousand in number, for various purposes, but most importantly as bloodmeals.

As they departed that morning, leaving into the White Waste, King Druthor looked into the sorceress's steely eyes and saw a person he did not trust.

CHAPTER TWO:
SNOW MEN

Gimirias Nardenon, grandmaster of the Blood Knights

Gimirias—or Imras, as people had called him since childhood—trotted at the head of the army, ascending the hills and leaving the black-nettled pines of the taiga behind. In time, they found themselves in the White Waste. Snow five feet deep stretched as far as he could see. Where white drifts of snow did not cover—their tops skirted with swirling white powder—giant blocks of ice drove through the inhospitable earth. Some people found it beautiful. Imras considered it hell.

His father had gone exploring, sent by the old king Drusion. He had never come back. Sometimes Imras wondered what had happened to him. He could have starved, but his father had been a tracker. He could find his way back from anywhere. No; something had taken his life. Something, in a land where everyone said there was nothing.

The temperatures steadily dropped as they went further into the White Waste. Part of it was the snow that now reached their hips; part of it was the approaching night, and part of it was their own unease.

Sometime as twilight set over the endless drifts of snow, casting the White Wastes pinkish-gold, a noise echoed throughout the hills—not a timber wolf or an elk, but clearly living—man-like, almost, but too loud for a man, and having no contours to the noise that indicated words. The Iron Sorceress, Liandré, gave a startled gasp.

It is good that she is afraid, Imras thought. *She will not try anything.*

Ahead of them, the tracker kept on. "Keep calm!" he snapped. Snow layered the wolf pelts and fox skins that covered his back. "There are dangers in the White Wastes. But the Snow Men, the abominable apes, only go after easy prey. They will not trouble a group so large.

They only attack men foolish enough to go alone."

Fool. Imras did not like the name applied to his father. But perhaps that was what he was. Or, perhaps, King Drusion just thought him expendable. And perhaps in Drusion's eyes, he was. But to Imras, growing up in the village of Agnon, his father had been everything to him. Not long before he died, Imras' mother had married the Lord of Agnon and the squalor of his father's hut had turned into the splendor of a stone mansion. His meals had gone from poached hare and common berries to rich crab roasts and endless goblets of wine or mead.

It was Drasanthi Nardenon, Lord of Agnon, that told him how the king sent his father away. In all, Drasanthi had not been unkind to Imras. Imras owed his position Blood Knight to him. But still… he wondered. He wondered why his mother had assumed so quickly that her husband was long gone. He wondered about Drasanthi Nardenon. And wondering would be the end of him.

Instead, he rode on through the drifts of thick snow and beside the wedges of pure ice, and paid respects to the father he had lost.

In the dark of the night, they set up camp. Sheltered from the wind by walls of ice, they huddled in the warmth of campfires. Imras sat near the tracker, envying his coat of pelts and hides, and casting glances into the crackling flame.

"I think the Snow Men killed my father," Imras blurted out. The words had weighed heavy in his mind, waiting to be spoken.

"It would not surprise me," the tracker said. "The Snow Men crave elven flesh more than anything. Even now, you can see them."

Up above the walls of ice, eyes glinted in shadow. Imras went cold, unable to breathe. Reflexively his hand went to the hilt of the sword.

"Do not worry." The flickering fire illuminated the tracker's smile. "There are at least a dozen Snow Men looking at us now. But you must understand—they are giants, and strong, and could likely defeat us if they are all united."

Imras had gone rigid as the ice around him.

"But they are not really men. They are nothing like us except in appearance. They are animals, my lord knight. One of them is more fearsome than a pack of wolves and either of us would die in single combat. But they are dumb. The only thing they care about is food, and they are afraid of fire. They will not trouble us, my good sir."

Despite his reassurances, the tracker's smile—illuminated in the flickering firelight—seemed to indicate he enjoyed Imras' dread. Perhaps the tracker saw in Imras what he had felt long ago, exploring the Wastes with his comrades. Surely in his less experienced years, when the tracker found his way to Danarion, taking the path he now led them on, he had felt as alone as Imras. Surely he, too, had felt he was going into the great dark where no one could hear them scream. Imras could hear the legends now, told in the taverns of Druenel-Hai… the lost army, led by King Druthor, never seen again. To find them, they would have to open the Snow Men's gullets. When Imras looked back up at the top of the white walls, more eyes glinted in the firelight. Dozens of Snow Men now watched them. Imras forced himself to look back into the fire. *I am a knight*, he told himself. *I should not be afraid.* But he had begun to wonder if he'd survive this mad journey after all.

CHAPTER THREE:
THE MOON DOOR

Gimirias Nardenon, grandmaster of the Blood Knights

Another day passed through the White Waste. Cold could not kill druen, but it hurt like hell, and Imras' steel plated armor burned when it brushed against his skin. He had already lost all feeling in his ears. Only at noon, when they stopped, and Imras drank a slave dry, did he have any respite from the freezing wind and heatless air. The warm blood filled his stomach and his veins, warming him, feeding him, and taking his mind far from the concerns of the present. In that moment, there was only blood.

They kept on through the giant snow-drifts. The soldiers often slipped on the icy ground, but Imras' steed Bloodmare was surefooted. The beast served him well always, and he loved her better than anyone else in the world, even more than his mother, or his stepfather the Lord of Agnon, or the woman he'd been pledged to marry. In the land of Nardur, you could trust no one save your pets. Even the lesser knights—behind a guise of deference and humility—strove constantly for a chance to steal his position. Imras knew it. He ran a hand through Bloodmare's hair, a coarse black on red, and looked on into the snow. The sun had begun to dip low. The hoarse cries of the Snow Men began again.

It would be a long night.

In the light of the campfires, Imras decided to sit next to someone new, someone besides the tracker whose words had racked him with chills. In the end, he chose the Iron Sorceress herself. Liandré, they called her. As he sat across from her, in the light of the crackling red flame, Imras regarded the beautiful nymphlike face, like a sculpture carved from ivory. Yet her eyes had a calculating look beneath the girlish façade, a look Imras also saw in the Black Zealots.

All magic-weavers are the same, Imras thought, *less trustworthy than anyone else in Varda.*

When he looked up again, Liandré's black eyes were boring into his. He wondered if she could read his mind. "You, there. Handsome. Do you have a name?"

I am pledged to be married, he reminded himself. But those eyes, that face, could drink men's souls like they drank his even now. "I am Imras." He hesitated. "Er—Gimirias, of the House Nardenon. A blood knight. Grandmaster, in fact." He sounded a fool. Beautiful women always did that to him. He cursed himself.

"The House Nardenon." Liandré's smile would be the end of him. "I would say I know it, but you would see it as a lie. I know little of your nation. But I am sure the House Nardenon is prominent..."

"Prominent in Agnon, certainly. As for the rest of the nation..."

"Do not be so modest," Liandré said. "It is not becoming of you."

"I am not being modest. I am being truthful."

"I see," Liandré purred.

Gods, that smile. "And if I am being truthful, you must be too," Imras went on. "Why did you tell us about Danarion being undefended? The Lonen hate the Lamen, yes, but that doesn't explain everything. Surely you want something from this. An iron sorceress like yourself doesn't do things for charity. And it is a long, long journey."

Liandré's catlike grin widened. "You are wise, Imras. Did you know that? The truth is that there are treasures for both of us in Danarion. There is a place in Danarion called the Tower of Warding where ancient tools of magic have been stowed away. The Iron Citadel has offered money in the past, but the proud western king refuses. By myself, I could not overcome the small garrison there. But with your help, I could slip in easily."

"Tools of magic, you say," Imras intoned. He wasn't sure he liked this woman after all. "Surely you could be more specific."

"The westerners have hidden away two of the three All-Seeing Orbs. In the hands of an expert sorceress, there is nothing his majesty King Aimon will not know. Nor the Iron Citadel. Every place in Varda will be under our eye."

"Two of three. Where is the third?"

In an instant, Liandré's smile was gone. "Some time in the aftermath of the Great War, it was lost. The last anyone knows, it was in the Dark Tower. It is probably destroyed."

Imras frowned. He had paid little attention to his tutors as a child. The Great War was a memory to all except the oldest of druen. Perhaps Druthor would know what the witch spoke of. But Imras, though grandmaster of the Blood Knights, dared not speak to the *drazzandori*... men had been impaled for much less. To enter his house without invitation was to offer oneself up as a bloodmeal; and even now, in the royal tent, Druthor remained alone with his bodyguard.

"Help!" a man shouted, and Imras stood up instinctively, hand going to the hilt of his sword. He drew in a cold breath.

The Iron Sorceress rose up out of the snow, staff in hand, graceful as a dove. In one of the faraway campfires, a Snow Man had grabbed a druen by the leg and now pulled him off into the darkness. Without hesitation Imras sprinted after him. The Iron Sorceress started a half second later and quickly overtook him.

The sight of the Snow Man was enough to undo a lesser warrior. The beast was nearly eight feet tall, covered in bright white fur except for its purple-skinned face. Two tusks stuck from its lips. Imras had the sword ready, and the air around the Iron Sorceress had the chill of magic. The edges of Imras' sword began to waver. He fell back a few steps. *I will not let her ruin my blade.*

But she had her eyes on others, thankfully. She thrust her hand forward and the soldiers by the fire—all six of them—no longer had swords. The metal blades smoked as they bent; they combined into a wavering ball of liquid iron, which suddenly stretched out like a spear, impaling the Snow Man as it ran away from its prey. Instantly, the Iron Sorceress relaxed her hands, and the weapon she had conjured fell to the snow as a useless ball of metal. The Snow Man fell on its back, and the snow around it turned red. Its prey—a druen soldier—ran up to the Iron Sorceress and clasped his hands together. "Oh, blessed one. I owe my life to you. I thought... I thought I was going to die."

"Be calm." Imras could hear her smile. "It is the least I could do."

The other soldiers—whose swords she had re-forged into useless metal—wore snarls on their faces. And when footsteps crunched through the snow behind him, Imras knew who was coming; and most importantly, he knew to back away, as quickly as possible without being noticed.

Druthor the Great himself, king of the vampires, arrived, his crimson robe standing out starkly from the white snow all around. "What is the meaning of this?" he hissed in that acidic voice Imras had come to fear. "That steel was well forged."

The Iron Sorceress turned around noiselessly, and if she feared Druthor she made no sign of it. "I saved a life."

"Ah, you saved a life," Druthor mocked her. "I have forgotten how the outlanders operate. Let me teach you a lesson, witch. I could have replaced that soldier there with a tenth of the money you lost me. Make that mistake again, and—"

"And you will not know where to find your grandfather's sword." The Iron Sorceress smiled wryly.

A few druen gasped. None had dared speak so impudently to their lord before.

"Do not worry, Your Majesty," the Iron Sorceress went on. "Just as I unmade their swords, I will remake them. They will not, perhaps, be as deadly as their predecessors. But they will do."

"You have much to learn about the druen, my sweet." Druthor's voice was surprisingly calm. "If you continue to disrespect your superior, you will regret it... sooner or later, you will wish you hadn't."

The Iron Sorceress continued to smirk. She obviously did not believe him, but Imras did. Druthor had won against more powerful foes. Indeed, anyone who could keep the Black Zealots in check was strong enough to best this southern witch.

"Very well," the Iron Sorceress said. "I have heard you out. We do not need to discuss this any longer."

"Watch yourself," Druthor intoned. "I do not make empty threats." He turned in a swirl of crimson and went back toward the royal tent.

The Iron Sorceress laughed coldly, raised her hands, and began reworking the swords she had ruined. Imras doubted they'd be half as good.

In the cold light of the following morning, in the near-blinding brilliance of the snow, Imras reflected on how far they still had yet to go. The Snow Men were nowhere to be seen, but such a long journey would be fraught with danger. *Months,* he thought to himself. *Months…*

A week in the White Wastes was hell enough for him. Eventually the cold and snow would get to him. *At least it is not winter,* he told himself, but even that was small comfort. *In the White Wastes there is no difference.*

A short while after noon, as dark clouds formed over the western horizon and threatened to steal the sunshine, the tracker stopped in the chill air. Imras, riding at the vanguard as always, sensed something amiss. The army stopped behind him.

The tracker turned around slowly. His always-sure eyes had the shallow look of worry. "We are being watched."

"Watched?" Imras snapped. "By whom?"

The tracker pointed toward a red speck in the distance. "The King keeps a menagerie of birds—"

"Ah!" There was no mistaking the Iron Sorceress's shrill voice. "We cannot—" Imras looked back; she was working her magic, sending a spear of iron toward the distant bird. "No! No! It is all in vain! We cannot let them know. They will be ready. We cannot let them be ready!"

"Witch. It will be three days or more before the bird has returned to his master," the tracker began, "but there is something. The Moon Door."

Her eyes widened; first, joy, then disbelief. "Truly? But how far is—"

"Not far," the tracker answered. "Two days, at most."

"What are you talking about?" Imras snapped.

"Two Moon Doors were built in ancient days," the Iron

Sorceress droned as if reciting a lesson, "one near the World Tree; another somewhere in the southlands. Walk through one and you will enter through the other. I thought it was mere legend. But you have found—"

"I know the White Wastes by heart," the tracker said. "I have found the site of the World Tree—though now it is only a great mound. And like all the books say, the Moon Door is there. I do not where it will lead us."

"Somewhere in the south," the Iron Sorceress said. "Somewhere much, much closer. And that is the best we can hope for, if one of the King's birds is already returning with the news."

The tracker nodded. "Indeed."

"The magic has likely faded already. But with enough effort…"

The tracker nodded again.

Moon doors and All-Seeing Orbs, iron witches and Black Zealots. Imras thought of home. It had its challenges, but at least he did not have to keep such dangerous company. Nothing good ever came from magic or those who weaved it. And to think he'd be a part of it, stepping through Moon Doors and helping the witch find her All-Seeing Orb… he shivered at the thought. But it was his duty, and a Blood Knight serves his liege to the end.

"We go south." The tracker's eyes met Imras'. "We must be careful. Even in the World Tree, there are dangers."

Tales of the World Tree had reached Imras in his childhood lessons. A tree whose trunk was large as a city, whose tip was near high as a mountain. The forces of darkness—with the help of the druen's ancestor, Gilden—burned it to the ground. It had been lost, everyone thought. The White Wastes were the last place Imras would have thought of looking.

CHAPTER FOUR:
THE WORLD TREE

Gimirias Nardenon, grandmaster of the Blood Knights

Dadryas, the World Tree, looked nothing like the stories said.

After traveling two days amid the biting winds and the cries of the Snow Men, they had arrived at what remained of the World Tree. Now it was a great white flattop hill—the decayed remains of a stump, perhaps, layered and layered in snow and ice—that stretched as far as Imras' eyes led. With the Iron Sorceress and the tracker, Imras rode at the vanguard.

"I do not understand," Imras said. "In the stories, the World Tree was in a garden of green. There were—"

"You do not understand." The Iron Sorceress did not look back at him, only kept riding. "Indeed, you do not. When the World Tree lay here, the world was warmer. It was warmer, and it was better. But the ice and snow have crept south. The Time of the Elves is long-gone, the westerners say. The Time of Mankind has dawned. The Time of the Elves was silver; the Time of Mankind will be steel."

"Humans are backward. They—" The Iron Sorceress cut him off before Imras could finish.

"Even now they grow in strength," the Iron Sorceress went on. "Far south, they make war on their Elvish masters. Soon their glory will outdo us—a glory of war and bloodshed, of steel rather than silver—but it does not matter. There is much you do not understand, Imras, but that is not my concern. My concern is to find the Moon Door."

Imras glared at her silken black hair. Then he gazed at the white flattop hill, and imagined an oak tree with a trunk the size of the city, hundreds or perhaps thousands of feet tall, and a garden of green that surrounded it where the ancients played music, sang, and pondered sacred mysteries. He longed for those days; but those days were gone, and Imras' ancestor Gilden had played a part in bringing about their end. Now the garden was iced-over; the glorious World Tree was only a flattop hill, the remains of a hacked-down stump, and the utopian age was gone with the wind of Time.

How far-gone is that time, Imras thought as the freezing wind cut into him like a cold dagger. Wedges of ice and billowing snow-drifts surrounded what once was a verdant paradise. Even the druen—riding behind Imras—being immune to death by cold, had a miserable look to their pale faces. Around and around they went, crossing the giant breadth of the flattop hill. Eventually a stone edifice, layered with tongues of ice and nearly overcome by an encroaching snow drift, appeared.

The Iron Sorceress cried out in delight, like a child offered a sweet. "It is real. It is real," she chanted. "The door made by the Wonder Smith himself... imbued with a power not seen since the prior age." She hopped off her palfrey and trudged through the snow. "Where will you take me?" she asked as if speaking to a person. "Where will you take us?" she corrected herself, and Imras cast a cautious glance backward.

King Druthor rode forth on his giant black charger, steering the beast along as it huffed and puffed fog. Instinctively Imras rode away from his path. Ahead of them, the Iron Sorceress approached the Moon Door, boots crunching against the snow.

The Moon Door was of dark gray stone, except for crescent-moons that dotted its sides, made of sparkling white crystal. Above, ancient symbols were etched above the lintel-like top, symbols Imras had seen before but did not understand.

"So this is how we will go south," King Druthor said.

The Iron Sorceress made no reply. She touched the end of her staff to one of the white crystal moons. "An ancient wonder, made by the great elvensmith himself, Danthelon Lunitar, who also forged the first *estirion* blades... like the very *estirion* blade you seek." She paused, as if in thought. "Reactivating this will sap all my strength. And even using everything I have, I will only provide a fraction of the power it needs; but with that little glimmer it will begin to work again." She turned around, for once acknowledging the druen-king's presence. "I will go in first, and see what lies beyond. Then when I feel it is time, I will come back, and give the command to enter. Do you understand?"

Druthor would not defer to her with as much as a nod. Instead, he stayed silent and glared; the most respectful affirmation the druen-king would afford her.

She turned around and placed the tip of her staff again on a white crystal moon. Then it all began to unfold. First the air chilled, growing cold but not in a way that made it uncomfortable; instead, it seemed to freshen. The faintly sweet scent of magic radiated from her staff, gooseflesh formed on Imras' skin, and then, little by little, the white crystal moon began to glow. First it was only a faint spark, but then, before Imras knew it, light burst from it like a star, and the Iron Sorceress cried out as if in pain. One by one, the other white crystal moons began to shimmer then burst into starlight. When all the white moons blazed with light, a sheet of white energy blazed from the stone edifice, forming a door of sorts, and the Iron Sorceress shrieked in pain, stumbling and then falling down on her back, panting and utterly spent.

Imras fell a few steps backward on his horse. He had seen the Black Zealots work their magic before, their transformations into monsters and their massacres of the *drazzandori's* enemies. He had seen Liandré, the witch herself, bend and alter metal. But he had never seen such brilliance, such a huge display of power, a blinding light that replaced the sun on this gloomy day. The Moon Door whined as the magic radiated, and Imras wondered if it would burst apart. But he knew the power of the ancients, the tools they created, could not be destroyed easily and certainly not by virtue of their own purposes. No, the door would operate as it had in the past. Imras looked back. King Druthor shielded his eyes from the light with his wizened grey hands. Behind, approaching the blazing luminescence, the Black Zealots were approaching—their gaunt, emaciated faces looking more dead than alive, the blood-crusted furs of beasts hanging over their shoulders, and bones, tied to cords, hanging around their chests as grim necklaces.

Ahead, the utterly spent Iron Sorceress was slowly but steadily getting up. "I will go see what lies beyond the door," she panted.

"Once I see it is clear, I will come back, and motion you inside."

The *drazzandori*, squinting, gave her a brusque nod. The Iron Sorceress half-walked, half-stumbled into the light, which consumed her; and she was gone.

"I do not trust her," Imras snapped. It was a thought that had collected within him a long time, but finally turned to words.

King Druthor met his gaze, half-squinting, and Imras wanted to flee from it. A king of the druen was, by necessity, cruel. Even for the grandmaster of the Blood Knights, it was best to keep one's mouth shut. But the stern father of the vampire race—to his surprise—gave a slight nod. It was more respect than he usually gave even to druen lords. "Nor do I, Gimirias Nardenon," Druthor said. "Nor do I."

Minutes later, the light of the Moon Door became erratic, bursting into light and then fading into a dim glow. The white crystal moons lost their star-like brilliance. *She is shutting the portal*, Imras realized. He had to act now before it gave out altogether. He clucked and kicked his shins into Bloodmare's sides. He raced into the portal. A beast rushed ahead of him, leaping in. They found themselves in a black tunnel.

Ahead of them was a light that could only be the other Moon Door. Its light, too, was fading. The beast—whatever it was—bolted ahead even faster than Bloodmare's gallop. Just as the light ahead was about to give out, Imras reached it, borne on the wings of Bloodmare's hooves, and plunged through the other side, back into the material realm.

CHAPTER FIVE:
THE TOWER

Gimirias Nardenon, grandmaster of the Blood Knights

On the other side of the Moon Door lay a darkened room. An orb of light, a star-gem, hanging from the wall served as the only light. In the dim illumination, the Iron Sorceress clutched an orb of blackish-green glass. Still perhaps disbelieving that any had followed, she stroked it with her ivory hands, muttering to herself: "Of course, Moon Door, you led directly to the Tower of Warding… of course, now I shan't have to deal with…" She looked up, and her eyes met Imras'. She gasped. "I thought I had gotten rid of the druen. You had outlived your use. There is no point in… Ah! Of all the druen I am glad it was you, the handsome Blood Knight. It is true, as a group the Iron Coven despises men, but I do not. I should like to take you back to the Iron Isle. Stranger things have happened than an Iron Sorceress wedded to a man."

I have to act carefully. She has total power over me, he reminded himself, knowing both he and his horse were covered in iron, the very thing she held power over. But in his silence, a low growl became evident. Standing knee-high to him was one of the most feared incarnations of the Black Zealots; he had transformed himself into a flesh hound, a skinless dog with raw red skin and hollow eyes, that sent even the most hardened druen into a panic.

The Iron Sorceress gave a startled gasp, but her surprise faded and her mouth pursed into a thin line. "Ah," she said, "if you shall come with me to the Iron Isle as my husband, I suppose we will have to take your pet dog as well…"

In a less tense situation, Imras would have laughed at her jest. Now, he could barely speak the words that came next: "Liandré, your honor, it is all very simple. I know we have outlived our use. You no longer need an army to get your orb… but I plead with you, I have ventured far to find *Lifedrinker*. I will not return without it. I beg of you…"

The Iron Sorceress gave a smug smile. "You scorn me. A great lady asks your hand in marriage, and you change the topic. Know, Imras, that the *estirion* sword you seek is here, in the Tower of Warding, though I am not sure where it is. It is no matter. I shall have you as my husband, or I shall have you as a corpse. Choose carefully."

"I am pledged to be married."

"A corpse, then?"

The growling of the flesh hound grew louder and louder by the moment. "Well… I suppose I will marry you then. But…" He surveyed his surroundings. The room was full of objects that looked like they had not been used in centuries, like a forgotten attic where ancient keepsakes collected dust. There were white staffs seemingly worked from bone; there were figurines of crystal or black ebony. There were books that had the ambience of magic emanating from them. The whole room had a feeling of heightened power, a center-point of magic pressure ready to explode. Imras did not want to test it. But the door was just there, and the knob was in reach of his hand.

"Shall we go, then?" the Iron Sorceress began. "Will you marry me, Gimirias Nardenon?"

Imras dismounted from Bloodmare. "Uhrm, yes," he said, and grabbed the doorknob.

The iron armor he wore slipped from him like skin peeled from an apple. The barding of Bloodmare was gone by the time he looked back; and a shimmering sphere of molten metal hung above them in the room. Imras had thought she was winded, but now the Iron Sorceress had dropped the All-Seeing Orb; her staff was back in her hand like it had never left, and if she was exhausted she was using the last bit of power.

"Try that door, and you will be sorry."

He twisted at it anyway, and a flurry of things happened all at once: a spear of iron jabbed from the molten sphere, piercing Bloodmare's heart; the sphere coalesced and then fell in a rain of iron spears, and the cage closed on top of Imras, as sturdy as any prison ever was. As soon as it happened, the flesh hound pounced her, raking its filthy, diseased claws into her tight black robe and exposing the skin beneath, which soon dripped with blood. She screamed, falling back against the stone wall, and in an instant Imras' prison had vanished into a long spear, poised to slay the flesh hound that troubled her.

Imras twisted the knob and ran. A wave of energy preceded him, a release of the chamber's latent magic. A shrill bell began to ring. Whoever, or whatever, guarded the Tower of Warding, knew there were intruders. Imras did not know whom to fear more: the Iron Sorceress or the guardians of the Tower of Warding.

~

As he ran through dark corridor after dark corridor, twisting through the mazelike network, Imras remembered he had his sword. Liandré had sucked his armor into her molten sphere of iron, but she had left his most prized possession, whether through genuine affection or obliviousness, he did not know or have time to guess. Instead he kept on through the tunnels, not knowing anything except that he needed to find *Lifedrinker*, the blade that belonged to the vampires by right.

Eventually, he broke free from the maze of hallways and corridors and found himself in a giant vault, lit dimly with star-gems dangling by golden chains. The tile floor spanned several hundred feet. And there were others here. Elven men—Lamen Elves, with long golden hair and blue or green eyes, leaf-shaped swords and long blue robes—paced around with the tense look of warriors who had never done their duty. Indeed, this was likely the first time someone had broken into the Tower of Warding, and from within. Imras did not know the outside of it, but he doubted it was possible to break in that way.

"Someone must have entered through a portal!" one of the warriors shouted. "The alarm was sounded from the storeroom..."

"The Moon Door!" another shouted. "Someone came from far away. What a powerful magician he must be! Be ready!"

The warriors ran toward one of the doors that faced the "storeroom." They had nearly all plunged into darkness when one turned and stopped, peering in Imras' direction. "Ah! I've found the rat! Your sorcery has no power on me… I have been warded!" By the time he'd finished talking their swords had kissed once. He cut swiftly but Imras answered each stroke of the blade with a parry, and the clangs echoed almost without pause. Imras drove him back toward the open space of the vault, always asserting himself, always pushing ahead and controlling the flow of the battle.

Back away, and you lose.

The warrior's leaf-green eyes widened as the light strengthened. "You are a druen! A blood-drinker in the Tower of Warding!"

A hard cut from Imras, and the warrior lost an arm. He staggered back, gushing blood onto the once-pristine tile floors. Another hard cut, and the warrior was armless, his sword skidding away from the lifeless grip. Even now, Imras hated death. At the sight of the crimson liquid, he fought an urge to drink. But he had a much more pressing concern: the weapon he had come for, *Lifedrinker*, ancient blade of the vampires. He had no idea where to find it. He had no idea where to look.

And out of the shadows, a dozen more Lamen warriors emerged, some with swords and a few with quarterstaffs. Even Imras, grandmaster of the Blood Knights, could not defeat a dozen warriors without help. They would cut him down. Imras thought of running, but that would only spell his doom even quicker. He swallowed and determined to back away. If he faced his death, he would face it with honor.

~

Dralynthi, Black Zealot

He ran, and he ran as the flesh hound.

The scent is strong, it thought. *The scent of the one I follow, and the scent of others.* The Iron Sorceress had wounded him but she had found herself in a different kind of trouble. *The scent strengthens*, it thought as it dashed through the dark hallways. *The scent of the one I follow, and of the ones whose blood I will drink.* As the flesh hound, senseless in its hunger, Dralynthi the Black Zealot found his way. The nose of the flesh hound never erred.

~

Gimirias Nardenon, grandmaster of the Blood Knights

Together, the elven warriors were a force that Imras could not overcome. A blade opened his arm, slashing deep into the flesh, and blood dripped onto his armorless body. He would blame the Iron Sorceress, but even fully prepared he doubted he could best these twelve warriors. They had skill and—though they wore little armor—their swords or staves cast any blow of Imras' aside before it could land. He was backing away, sure to loose, when the flesh hound arrived.

Skinless, looking like it belonged in a butchery rather than dashing around, clawed and bit its way through the crowd of warriors, leaping from one victim to the next and spraying more blood onto the already-reddened floors. Soon, most of the warriors had fallen to its fury—all but one, running away as fast as he could—when Imras screamed, "Stop!"

To his surprise, the flesh hound listened. It shifted shape until it had become the Black Zealot again—a bone-thin druen with beady eyes, having discarded his fur robe during the transformation. Imras did not like those deep-socketed eyes staring at him, or looking at him at all.

The Lamen warrior had dropped his sword, and Imras ran after him. He bounded across the room and grabbed the warrior as he ran, restraining him. This was a guard from the Tower of Warding, and even better, a coward.

He held him fast as the Black Zealot approached in the dim light, tall and gangly, his nakedness revealing protruding ribs and skeletal thinness.

"Would you like to live—?"

"Lunesti," the warrior whimpered.

"Lunesti," Imras continued. "The Black Zealots do not believe in mercy like you westerners do. You will tell me, Lunesti, what you will know. Or you will wish you had joined your brothers-in-arms."

The mess of blood and bodies made Imras' stomach turn, but the flesh hounds delighted in slaughter.

"Whatever you want to know," Lunesti breathed, "I will tell you."

"Where is *Lifedrinker*, the *estirion* blade that belonged to my grandfather Gilden?"

The Black Zealot had grown close, too close for even Imras' comfort, gliding across the tile floor with the grace of a dancer. Those beady black eyes held no compassion for Lunesti, certainly, but they had none for Imras either.

"*Lifedrinker*. Gilden. Ah, I think I know," Lunesti whimpered.

Not good enough.

"The castellan of the Tower of Warding keeps everything he wants to hide in the storeroom. It is a mess there, and hard to find things, but I assure you your grandfather's blade can be found there."

Imras exhaled, and the anger welling up inside him made him tighten the grip on Lunesti. *All this time wasted. Perhaps the iron witch has already stolen it.* "Gods damn you." He cast Lunesti to the floor and broke into a run. He wondered what the Black Zealot would do with the cowardly Lamen warrior. He realized, after all, that he did not care.

In an instant, he was back in the twisting corridors again, but this time he was calm enough to navigate. The shadowy halls of the Tower of Warding led him slowly but inevitably back to the place his journey began.

CHAPTER SIX:
THE CONFRONTATION

Gimirias Nardenon, grandmaster of the Blood Knights

He was in sight of the storeroom when the flesh hound dashed by, fresh blood dripping from its skinless red muzzle. The Iron Sorceress stood there. At the sight of her, Imras dropped his sword; in her presence it would only work against him.

Liandré was panting hard. If she had not been spent before, she was spent now. An orb of iron, solidified, no longer wavered in the air; it had fallen to the ground. And before her, a stone giant lay in pieces. *The Guardian of the Tower*, Imras wondered, *or perhaps just a guardian.*

The flesh hound was bending its sinewy muscles, ready to pounce and rip out her throat, when Imras screamed, "Stop!" and, again, the beast obeyed. This time, it did not turn back into a Black Zealot; it remained its fleshy self, hovering around her with an ever-present growl.

Sweat layered the Iron Sorceress's pallid skin. Her breathing was strained and labored. She fell back against the wall, just barely managing to hold on to her staff.

"I am the greatest magic-weaver on the Iron Isle. I could likely challenge the High Sorceress," she rasped, "but I have opened an ancient way-gate, and disrupted a Stone Guardian. Know that there are more coming, Gimirias my sweet. I would shut the door, if you value your life."

For once, he trusted her words. He slammed it shut, and looked down at his own arm. He had bled all over his shirt. And he was just as exhausted as the Iron Sorceress. He slumped against the door. "The sword is in here."

The Iron Sorceress made no reply, only panted.

In the dim illumination of the star-gem, Imras breathed deep and slow. The shadowy shapes of the objects all blended together. But eventually he left his place and began to search.

A while later, the form of a sword, propped up in the corner, caught his eye. The light was dim but there it was, behind the now-useless Moon Door, a sword of blackish-gray metal leaned against the wall. A skull was forged over the crossbar. When he laid his hands around the hilt, and lifted it up in the dim light, he knew he had found the ancient treasure of his ancestor. He kissed the flat of *Lifedrinker*, and burned his lips with cold.

He had found what he wanted. But there was a problem. He was hundreds, perhaps thousands of miles from where he needed to be. King Druthor likely still waited in the freezing wastes where they'd left him. His only hope was the Moon Door. And only the Iron Sorceress knew how to imbue it with magic again.

When he met her dark eyes, her trembling lip and whitening face indicated she knew what he intended her to do, and that she did not want to do it.

"Liandré," Imras said, "You know what you need to do."

"And I will not, because I cannot," Liandré hissed. "There is not enough power in my body left. It would kill me."

Imras pointed *Lifedrinker* at her. "Then you have a choice of deaths."

Liandré hissed and lifted her hands. The air took on a telltale sweet chill. And at the feel of it, the Black Zealot lost control.

~

Dralynthi, Black Zealot

He attacked, and he attacked as the flesh hound.

She is vulnerable, it thought, and *I crave her blood*. It was on her, then, fangs sinking through the already-torn black cloth, jaw clenching tight. And then, a harsh puncture; iron ripping through flesh, through its sensitive skinless body. He had underestimated her, and he had underestimated her as the flesh hound.

~

Gimirias Nardenon, grandmaster of the Blood Knights

A yelp echoed through the room, so wretched it could only be the flesh hound. She had bent the once-solid iron ball, caused a spike to emerge that impaled the skinless dog like meat on a hook. Now she had truly spent every bit of what she had left. She fell against the wall harder than she ever had, covered so thickly in sweat it looked like she had just bathed. Her breath was so strained it sounded like the last gasps of a dying woman. She had no power left; she was utterly at Imras' mercy.

"*Lifedrinker* will not be kind to you if you do not listen." Imras smiled. "You will open the Moon Door, or I will slice your throat."

"A knight killing a woman. I have not heard of such things."

"Then you have not met the Blood Knights. I will not have you transport me thousands of miles, and then abandon me when the mission is complete. I will kill you if you do not obey." Imras wondered if he was bluffing.

"I have seen worse behavior from the vampires. It would not surprise me in the slightest." Her eyes, though shallow with fear, held a familiar condescension: the condescension of a powerful sorceress, a great woman, a noble lady, speaking to someone far beneath her station. To the Lonen and the Lamen and all the other tribes, the druen were scum, if they were ever mentioned at all.

Imras ground his teeth together. "There are Lamen warriors here, woman. Tens of thousands, probably, in this city. I cannot defeat an army. But if you will not open the Moon Door, I suppose I can enjoy one last bloodmeal."

The Iron Sorceress cried out as if struck.

Someone pounded on the door. "Open at once!" someone shouted from outside in a Lamen accent. "The King wants you dead or alive! If you resist, it will be the former!"

"Ah," Liandré panted, chest heaving with breath. "Gimirias of the House Nardenon, I will open the Moon Door under one condition."

"I will hear no conditions," Imras growled.

"I want your kiss on my lips."

In an instant Imras obeyed. It was a small concession and one—when he performed it—he did not mind in the slightest. She knew how to kiss, how to draw a man in, and Imras felt his blood warm, felt his body respond to her grasping hands. And then he pushed away, though he did not want to. For the first time, he realized the Iron Sorceress—beyond all her condescension and high status— had all the weaknesses and emotions of those beneath her. Tears streaked from her black huntress's eyes, but she turned dutifully toward the Moon Door, touched her staff to a white crystal moon, and began her work with a scream of pain.

For a half-second Imras fought guilt, working Liandré to death, but he reminded himself this was the woman who had tricked them, who had slipped halfway across the world and intended to leave the druen in the cold. Guilt, he remembered, is a feeling that druen by necessity should learn to ignore.

As the white crystal moons filled with light, the Iron Sorceress's body weakened, growing bone-thin. Her knees wobbled, threatening to give in at any second. Tears flowed again, not from love anymore but now from the sheer pain of her task, the pain written all over her grimacing face and trembling hands. In time the screams stopped, becoming a gurgle and then a whimper and then a whine. Seconds later, the white crystal that dotted the Moon Door blazed with a flickering light, and a sheet of white energy filled the open space, not as powerful as before and threatening to give out at any moment.

In the same moment Liandré dropped to the floor, perhaps dead or perhaps unconscious. *It does not matter*, Imras reminded himself. He looked down at what his white fingers grasped—the blade, wrought from dark grayish metal, a skull forged upon its hilt, the ancient heirloom of the vampires, *Lifedrinker*—and remembered that it was the only thing that mattered. A Blood Knight serves his liege unto the end. Despite his best efforts he looked down at the still body of Liandré. The door at last opened, and Lamen warriors poured in. The white sheet of the Moon Door flickered, threatening to evaporate any moment.

Imras bolted forward and ran, completing a journey of many

months in the blink of an eye.

CHAPTER SEVEN:
VAMPIRE BLADE

Druthor the Great, King of the Vampires

The Blood Knight burst from the portal, just as Druthor was ready to give the signal, as he was ready to turn around and head toward Druenel-Hai in defeat. In the knight's hands was a sword not of common iron, but darkish-gray, with the skull-forged hilt he remembered. The knight hit the floor, panting as he knelt in the snow. Druthor pushed him aside and laid his hands around the hilt. And then, looking at the perfect craftsmanship, he—despite everything he'd learned from ruling the druen race—began to smile.

For nearly a hundred years, it had been outside of druen hands. Now the weapon was his, its hilt grasped tight in spindly white fingers. The druen nation would live strong and prosper forever.

And this blade will drink the lives of those who oppose it.

"My lord!" The Blood Knight's hands were clasped together. "What is my reward?"

"Reward," Druthor laughed. "When my grandfather wielded this sword, he would reward men by not killing them. But you, Blood Knight, shall have whatever you ask for."

He turned and led the procession as it wound its way north and east.

~

Druthor, *drazzandori*, King of Nardur and father of the vampire race, took his rightful seat at the Crimson Throne. By his request, the Blood Knight stood guard at his right hand, having forsaken the name Nardenon.

A king, he was, on the Crimson Throne; but he was the first true lord of the vampire race, for in his hands lay *Lifedrinker*. The corrupting wind that once plagued Nardur, rusting swords and ploughshares, was long-gone and long-forgotten; but a new wind blew, a wind not of magic but of mind, a sense that the vampire race would rise to strength and subdue the world.

~

From the halls of the Black Castle and its Crimson Throne, this wind of mind blew in all directions. News spread from the king's innermost court to the furthest village: the ancient blade of the vampires had returned to its rightful place, and this good wind of fortune could only mean that greater things were yet to come; that the vampire race would rise up once more as a great army of darkness to rule Varda, and, in time, every elven nation would call the *drazzandori* its lord.

CRIMSON THRONE

Loud hollow bells clanged from the towers of Druenel-Hai, and their message was clear: "The King of the Druen is dead!" Across the main thoroughfare, a group of slaves ferried the ancient lord of the vampires—his corpse at rest in a long black coffin—to its place of interment. As the procession neared the Library of Druthor, where the late king had stowed books of forbidden knowledge and old history, heralds rode out from every city gate. One went east toward the sea; another west into the taiga; and another south, toward Sardur where the Hill Ghouls lived. The northward-bound herald would stop at every town of significant size, but he would not venture far from the road. The Lonely Temple already knew everything that went on, and no sane man would go where the Black Zealots had their home.

~

Drasanthi Giltharion, Black Zealot

A fire blazed on the black stone floor of the Lonely Temple. Around it, Drasanthi and his dark brothers danced and shifted forms. One moment, Master Drudar was the Flesh Hound—skinless and red—and then in an instant he became the Bone Devil, its spiny tale full of venom. Drasanthi felt himself change every moment, though he did not know who or what he became. A portentous event had happened, Master Drudar said, and it was time for the zealots to enter their *ecstasy*.

Master Drudar was the Wolf Man, now, a thick mane of black hair covering his wolfish head on an otherwise druen body. Marsané had become the Flesh Hound—though a woman she was a brother, for among the zealots there was no male or female—and then she was the Skinned Witch, red and raw with tentacle hair and blazing yellow eyes.

"From the place of darkest darkness, knowledge cometh!" Master Drudar howled as the Wolf Man. "The king is dead and with his passing, the worst time yet shall fall upon us! But if the right man achieves the Crimson Throne, then shall our iron kingdom become true steel. *So saith the darkest darkness!*"

"So saith the darkest darkness!" Drasanthi howled as the Wolf Man.

"So saith the darkest darkness!" Marsané chittered as the Bone Devil.

"So saith! So saith!" Master Drudar screamed as the Skinned Witch, and lifted her bloody stumps of hands.

The fire burst, sending a jet of flame into the sky and leaving a pile of ash and human bone. The *ecstasy* was complete.

"From the darkest darkness comes the truth!" Master Drudar howled as himself.

CHAPTER ONE:
AN EVENTFUL EVENING

Homar of House Allenon, Lord of Samarion

When the herald began shouting his message in Samarion, Lord Homar had just returned from his daily hunt. The black walls of Druenel-Hai rose above the sea of dark pines where Lord Homar engaged in his favorite pastime, and while chasing his quarry the bells—though faint—had echoed even through the isolated forest. He had already drunk his prey dry, and left the slave's corpse in the woods for the wolves.

A rare summer snow drifted down as the herald continued shouting: "His majesty, the revered King Druthor the Great, has passed away from the world of the living."

Homar smiled. In his twilight years, the nearly three hundred-year-old Druthor had hired the greatest alchemists from throughout the elven world, asking them to create an elixir of life. His only goal, as his body gave way to age, was to live forever. The alchemists had tried all sorts of ingredients—from lead to mercury, from dulled arsenic to the flesh of exotic beasts—but nothing could help his steadily worsening health. Homar wondered if Druthor the Great had poisoned himself on his quest to live forever. At the thought, he laughed, and a few of his subjects looked back at him in surprise. In response, he snarled; he had hanged people for less.

"He has not left a will. However, in accordance with the customs of our great nation, the Crimson Throne shall go to Dorrias, his eldest son by his first wife."

Homar had not heard the name Dorrias in a long time. He had faded from the memory of most Lords of Nardur. But Homar would respect the law, he decided. The Lords of Nardur held each other in check, and, as long as Dorrias made no changes, he would not contest his rule.

That night, in the feasting hall, Homar and his wife ate their usual dinner of fish—this time, crab roast in the style of Port Andom—and began their dinner with the usual idle talk, but those were the only things usual about it. In the distance, over the dark walls of Druenel-Hai, the unmistakable glow of fire emerged. A column of smoke wafted upwards.

The capital city of Nardur, burning. Lord Homar shivered.

"I wonder who has attacked," his wife spoke in hushed tones, "and on the king's death-day."

Lord Homar kept his reserve of knights always at the ready. The morning would bring news. And with the news, he would make his decision.

CHAPTER TWO:
THE CITY IN FLAMES

Lunitari, Slave

Three strokes of the sword, and three sharp parries with his staff. The invader drove Lunitari steadily backward. These men had come into the gates without warning, and the gates had been opened for them. More proof—besides the white skin and pointed ears of the soldier before him—that druen, not outsiders, were attacking. But who would lay siege to their own city, burn houses and shops? Who had such little honor and integrity? Lunitari supposed that the druen, at heart, only served themselves. Back home, such a thing would be unthinkable. But then again, back home, most things Lunitari saw here every day would be unthinkable.

Perhaps this was his chance to escape. But an escaped slave was punished more horrendously than the vilest of murderers and parricides. The druen had lost their way, a priest in his home village had said. Lunitari had been such a fool to travel to Port Andom. And now, even after he paid the price for his folly, he was hesitant to flee.

Two more strikes, and Lunitari answered with his quarterstaff, striking twice as hard. At last he knocked the sword out of the druen's hand. He went in hard, as his training told him. He moved in for the trip...

A horn blew, rattling the walls. The burning roofs of the houses illuminated banners, coming fast inward: a black bat against a red field, the symbol of Lord Elras.

The druen warrior from before came running back, sword again in his hand. Lunitari struck hard with the quarterstaff, knocking the weapon again once more, and ducked into an alley. Lord Elras—or "Elras the Impaler" as some called him—would surely overcome the old king's forces. And then, the ancient vampire lord would surely take the Crimson Throne and proclaim himself the *drazzandori*.

In the shadows, Lunitari waited, pondering his next move. Hundreds of people—druen subjects and slaves of all kinds—ran with buckets of water to put out the blaze. *It is summer*, Lunitari remembered, *and the Black River flows*. If Lunitari followed a mere mile he'd reach the port. But Lunitari had blond hair, unlike any free druen, which would surely mark him as a slave. If he ventured across the infamously wild land of Sardur and somehow achieved the impossible task of reaching Port Andom, then would the elves there be any kinder than the druen?

He could still remember that fateful summer night more than three years ago. He had come to the port as an adventurer, seeking whatever employment he could attain, and this… this was how it had ended. It was only his skill with the staff and longknife—his skill in *dó kentas*, the ancient martial art of the Lamen Elves—and his undying loyalty to King Druthor, proven over and over again, that kept him alive. Most slaves were lucky to last two months before becoming bloodmeals. But through faithful service, honesty, and unflinching obedience—the very things Lunitari found absent in the druen around him—he had preserved his life. Until now, at least.

Now, Lord Elras had come from the northern region he presided over. Lunitari would be cautious as possible. Druthor, for all his shortcomings and vices, had rewarded loyalty. *Even among the worst of people, there is a trace of the Light*. And the Light had preserved Lunitari thus far; it was anyone's guess how much longer he would last in this land of shadow.

The horns pealed again, sending a shudder through Lunitari. He wondered if Lord Elras would reward loyalty like Druthor, but he doubted it, and it seemed unwise to take that chance. Elras' army was pouring in, though, and Lunitari had to find a way out. The gates were often shut for the night. He would have to use what his masters had taught him when he was only an initiate of *dó kentas*. He rushed through the alleyway toward the wall.

The staff is the most ancient weapon, his master had said. *It has the most uses of any tool. It is all you need.* But Lunitari still kept his longknife. The staff could trip and injure, but nothing ended an evildoer's life as quickly as a blade to the heart.

At a house near the wall, Lunitari put his hands and feet to use. With the window as leverage, he heaved himself high and used the uneven, protruding stone as handholds. A minute later, he stood on top of the roof. The dark stone wall of Druenel-Hai stretched another five feet above the roof. It was a risk Lunitari would have to take. He sprinted across the roof, and at the last moment, slammed his quarterstaff on the tile, heaving himself through the air. He struck the wall, grasping the bare edge of the wood battlements, which groaned under his weight. Little by little, he pulled himself up until, at last, he lay there on the uneven wood.

Behind him, the water-bearers had put out much of the fire. But at the north gate, lines of soldiers still poured in. Lunitari had forgotten how many soldiers the vampire lord had under his control. But now Lord Elras would sit on the Crimson Throne and Lunitari had no doubts his rivals would begrudge him.

In the city square—in the fading light of the last burning house—Lunitari could make out a pair of steel-armored guards escorting the former royal family out of the castle. Sitting on a litter, Lord Elras made a motion, and the guards moved in with swords. Lord Druthor's wife, his sons and daughters, all began to fall.

It is a black day, Lunitari thought, *a day of treachery and betrayal.* But treachery and betrayal were the norm in this land where the shadow lay so heavy. The land of the druen did not know the Light. Lunitari thought of home. He thought of the serene apple orchards on the coastal town where he lived. Then he looked back at the town square, and witnessed the beheading of Halé—Druthor the Great's sixth wife, whom Lunitari had grown to love like a sister—and realized he had to see justice done. But where would he go, and whom would he turn to? He knew the answer, though it troubled him. The Lords of Nardur would only serve themselves. As vile a reputation as they had, the Black Zealots were the key to resolving this madness. They alone had the power to subdue the druen lords.

Lunitari wondered if he was a fool not to run. But as *dó kentari* he held one principle above all others: to serve his liege with undying loyalty. And he could sense what Druthor the Great would want, though now he surely faced Judgment: *Avenge me*, Lunitari. *See that the true king is crowned.* And for those wishes to be carried out, Druthor's only hope was the very group everyone feared: Black Zealots in the Lonely Temple. In their dark madness, they had gained wisdom supreme.

CHAPTER THREE:
BLACK WIDOW

Sindomas of House Samsani, Lord of Belarras

"This shall not stand," Sindomas hissed, and slammed his white fist onto the table. Before him, two rulers of nearby regions—Lord Malthari "the Slayer" and Lady Narité "the Black Widow"—did not look half as angry. But the light of the Ebon Tower was faint as always, making it impossible to tell for certain how impassioned everyone was. "The threats of the other lords have always kept us all in check... stopped our country from falling into civil war. And now Lord Elras... that bat-eating, decrepit old man..." His skill at insults had faded with age. "...he has brazenly stolen the Crimson Throne, right under our noses..." His old heart sputtered at the thought. "Yet do we have enough to challenge him? Do we have enough soldiers to even surround the city as it is?"

"We do not," Lady Narité said in her loud whispering voice. "But perhaps I know how to get one."

The air cooled. For once Sindomas was grateful for the dark, windowless Ebon Tower, built by the first king Drusion in the madness of old age. Only a madman would build a watchtower with no windows, but Sindomas for once thanked the gods above and below for the Drusion's senility.

He did not want to see her face. Though the question of how to gain strength was on his mind he did not speak it. Narité answered the question without his prompt. "With enough death, I can create a kind of life."

A euphemism if I ever heard one. "So the rumors are true about you. You are a necromancer."

Though the light was nearly imperceptible, Sindomas could sense Narité's smile. "Yes, I am a magician, a worker of wonders... a merchant of the bizarre, and I deal in death. You may hear a rumor among my subjects that my husband has returned from the grave, so great was his love for me. The rumor is true in part."

The hand of magic, when it touched a druen babe, most often led him to the Lonely Temple and the path of the Black Zealot. But recorded among the annals in the Library of Druthor, the ancient texts and the forgotten tomes, were other gifts among vampire magic-weavers... powers of vanishing and instant journeys, powers of black ice or hellfire, and yes, powers of death.

"I sense that you do not believe me," Narité said.

"I do!" Sindomas said suddenly, too suddenly, perhaps giving away his fear.

"Behold, I shall wither this weakling!" Narité hissed.

Malthari had a bare second to gasp and fall back before the Black Widow worked her magic. Green light shimmered around her bony white fingers. Cracks formed on Malthari's skin—veins, Sindomas realized as they swelled, blue and green and thickening as his skin sunk in on itself. Yet it was the look in Narité's eyes that stole Sindomas's breath and made him fall backward: eyes black and devoid of human emotion, soulless black marbles that nonetheless burned with a twilight gleam.

A furtive glance back at Malthari and the former lord had lost what little color was left in his skin. Blackish-blue veins stuck out against white flesh like silty rivers in a snowy wasteland. The room became colder, thicker, more congested, and gooseflesh ripped across Sindomas' skin; he began to shake, and then, in an instant, it was over.

"Not only a necromancer," Narité laughed. The heaviness of the room vanished but Sindomas still shook. "A great one."

Sindomas ground his teeth together, trying to regain his composure. "Very well, Narité, black widow. But in all you have not proven your use. Your spells would work well against a helpless victim like Lord Malthari but against an army I am not so certain. A Blood Knight would have your head before you had even begun to weave your power..."

"Do not speak of things you do not understand." The voice was high pitched but undoubtedly masculine.

Sindomas glanced back and saw no other males within the Ebon Tower. But when he looked ahead everything made sense: Lord

Malthari staring back at him, bone-thin and rigid, his finger bones sticking far out of the swollen dead flesh. His eyes had become yellow, jaundiced, his teeth grown large in the wake of receding gums. And a cold billowed out from "Lord Malthari"—or the wicked creature that lived behind Lord Malthari's eyes—and it was not a cold borne of frost, but of malice and cold hunger.

"Lord Malthari has been a naughty thing." The Black Widow's ancient wrinkled face twisted into a smile. "He deserved it."

Sindomas wondered how on earth seven husbands had endured her, even for the short while before their deaths, now that he knew who she was. *But she is just a tool,* Sindomas reminded himself. *She is just a pawn in the game.* A pawn that could easily overpower him man-for-man, yes, but he remembered a saying from some ancient book: "A wizard has more to fear from a knife in the dark than all the world's armies converging upon her." There were many things Sindomas—though he was lord of Belarras—could not procure. A knife in the dark was not one of them, whether wielded by himself or an underling. He would use the wicked hag until she outlived her use and became a danger; then, as quickly as he had taken the pawn to the board, he would remove it. Or so he told himself, but as he peered into Narité's twilit eyes he wondered if he was a match for her at all.

"Lord Malthari has been a naughty thing," the Black Widow repeated at a purr, "but he has found a new use. I have remade the new Lord Malthari for war, even as I remade my seven husbands for love."

Seven husbands. The thought repeated in his mind. Seven husbands reclaimed from the grave. The Black Widow had earned her nickname. Sindomas' stomach turned.

At the base of the Ebon Tower, in the midst of the swirling powdery snow, Lord Sindomas stepped into the light of day. The Black Widow's slaves had already procured her horse from the stables. With each of her movements, they flinched. Elves, they were—nine in immediate view—and clearly not druen. Likely they had been picked from far south beyond the lifeless waste, and if they had been off the Andomasi slave-boats for more than a month they were lucky to be alive.

The fat woman heaved herself onto the saddle of her draft horse with surprising ease. She wheeled around to face him. Her pudgy, wrinkled cheeks, her piercing brown eyes, and her wisps of dark hair, seemed less ugly to Sindomas and more frightening. A toad, she was— as Sindomas' friends had called her—but a toad that all druen should fear. When one of her slaves handed her a knob-covered staff affixed with a black stone, Sindomas wondered why he had been such a dense fool. Of course, Lady Narité was a wizard.

I intend to use her as a tool, Sindomas reminded himself as his own slaves pulled their master's horse toward him by the reins. *But if I do not act wisely, I will become her slave.*

Narité's wolfish smirk grew into a smile. "In time it will be King Sindomas sitting on the Crimson Throne."

That had not been his intent.

"And beside him shall reign Queen Narité."

I shall not become the Widow's eighth victim, Sindomas promised himself, and wondered if, by joining her, he had made a terrible mistake.

CHAPTER FOUR:
DUTY

Lunitari, Slave

The freedom of the forest had its benefits—the fresh water of the stony brooks, the shade of the black-needled pines, and the quiet beauty of the meadows—but it also had its dangers. Though much of Nardur had traces of civilization, in the wilds a band of crazed wanderers called the Morthen searched for easy bloodmeals. Then there were, of course, the wolves, which troubled the druen as much as any other people; the brown bears that only an expert hunter could defeat; and other untold dangers that the nation of vampires hid within its great expanse. Whenever fear touched him, he reminded himself of *dó kentas*, the "way of the staff," and the many sayings his teacher had made him memorize to stave off fear.

The greatest thing mortal-kind fears is death; and death is only a release, a transformation into Light. Still, whenever a branch rustled to reveal a bird flying away, Lunitari felt himself go cold, felt his hands instinctively tighten round the quarterstaff, having doubts about all the platitudes his teacher forced him to learn. Among the druen, there was no concern about the afterlife. The southlanders—the Lonen—fervently denied its existence. But to the druen, they neither believed nor disbelieved. It seemed to a druen the only concern was one's own betterment. And occasionally Lunitari wondered if the vampires had it right; if there was nothing except what lay around him, nothing except strength and weakness, wealth and poverty, a battle—as a Lonen author once wrote—between the self-interests of all. Yet in his time Lunitari had seen bad folk get their justice and good folk rewarded. But it did not concern him at the moment. Now what concerned him was the restoration of the monarchy, honor and duty to his liege—more things the druen did not care for.

To the unlearned the Black Zealots would seem like fiends, but in truth, their efforts to keep away from the void, the shadow-realm that tempted all wizards yet invariably sent them into madness, had given them more of a moral compass than the druen lords. The zealots would know what to do. The zealots inspired fear, wrought havoc and violence, but Lunitari had no doubts they would welcome an honest visitor.

The journey lasted three days. The first day Lunitari braved bitter wind and snow—a day that belonged in winter, not mid-summer. Throughout the second and third, the clouds parted and gave way to the sun, yet the air retained its chill. At home, Lunitari recalled basking in summer's warmth. Now he couldn't even remember what it felt like to be warm. The thought of home made his eyes water, but it was a hope that needed to be dashed—and dashed it was, as soon as Lunitari beheld the Lonely Temple.

~

The grim gray pillars of the temple upheld a pyramidal roof, and a frieze of skulls and crossbones ran along it. The building itself stood alone in a sea of heathland, shrub-pines and rocks. No trees grew near it, and it seemed to Lunitari—as he pushed through—that they peeled back before the Lonely Temple's awesome gloom. It was easy to see why the Black Zealots inspired fear. And in truth, Lunitari felt a bit of it himself. His grip on his quarterstaff had grown so viselike his fingers had begun to sweat.   But he knew if he was polite and respectful, the zealots would tolerate him, or at least hear what he had to say.

No longer hidden in the pines—walking out among the open fields—Lunitari felt naked and exposed, as if a hundred thousand eyes were watching him with predatory gazes, waiting for him to make a misstep, for their chance to pounce. But little by little, the gray stone of the Lonely Temple grew closer. And when he had come within a dozen yards, a zealot emerged from the darkness.

Gray fur lined his long black robe. In height he was taller than anyone Lunitari had ever seen, yet in weight Lunitari would guess the zealot was half that of his kindred. In appearance, he resembled the druen of tall tales his grandmother had used to scare him: a face so thin it looked skeletal, eyes beady yet hungry, approaching gracefully yet uncertainly, as if walking was a dance to him.

Lunitari tried to say, "Greetings!" but a lump had formed in his throat, so hard he couldn't speak.

"A blond-haired Lamen comes to the Lonely Temple wielding nothing but a stick and a longknife."

Lunitari wanted to correct the Black Zealot, tell him the staff is the only weapon a true elf needs, and the most ancient, but now was not the time to repeat *dó kentari* platitudes.

"Stranger things have happened, I am certain," the Black Zealot went on, "but I cannot remember any. I am Drudar, highest ranking of our order. And what is your name, you fragile blond-haired thing?"

Lunitari probably weighed twice as much as this Drudar, and most of it muscle, but he would not argue. "My master was King Druthor. I served him loyally to my dying breath. I will continue to serve him if it is in my power."

"But it is not in your power, Lunitari," Drudar intoned, stepping ever closer with unpredictable birdlike strides. "The great pretender, 'King' Elras, has burned the will. He has sentenced anyone that speaks against him to immediate execution."

Lunitari frowned. "I thought you could help. I thought you would have answers."

"A fool, you are," Drudar laughed, "but a wise fool. I cannot help you." Drudar's body began to twist in shape and Lunitari gasped. Drudar's skin turned pinkish red, and as his muscles swelled, the black cloak burst at the seams and fell wisplike to the ground. Drudar's face became that of a hairless wolf: hairless except for the black mane that grew from his head and fell all around his shoulders. "But I can," Drudar—or what once had been Drudar—continued the thought. "Lord Elras thought he killed all Druthor's family. But he is terribly wrong. The king's son Dorrias, the crown prince himself, remains alive. The heir to the kingdom has been hidden away all these years. He is in the village of Drastheon-by-the-Sea, where his father kept him safe. If you go to the Manor there, and inquire for him, they will let you visit the heir to Nardur."

Lunitari turned to leave, thinking perhaps at last he had his chance to run.

"Do not leave yet." When he looked back Drudar had become himself again, his clothing nevertheless discarded. Now naked, his skeletal thinness seemed even more unnatural, and Lunitari drew in a cold gasp. "I knew you were coming, Lunitari. The Black Zealots are always well prepared. I have seen your arrival in visions, during the *ecstasy*... Go, Lunitari, to find the crown prince, and fortune will be with you. I shall watch your progress with delight."

The zealot's beady black eyes seemed to grow in intensity. Lunitari turned and sprinted down the road, quarterstaff in one hand and longknife in the other. *Drastheon-by-the-Sea*. The words echoed in his mind. A village of small import, certainly, for Lunitari had never heard the name before. But behind its obscurity hid the rightful heir to Nardur; and Lunitari could not help but do his duty.

CHAPTER FIVE:
THE KING'S RIGHTS

Homar of House Allenon

Lord Homar had picked out the perfect slave—a thin, waiflike human overcome with trembling—and he had already led his hunting horse from the stables. The morning hunt promised to be as delightful as any he remembered when a distraction arrived: a druen galloping in from the west. A rich scarlet cloak flapped behind him and the thick, dark gray plates of his armor indicated wealth, but even without all the finery Homar would recognize him.

"Lord Homar!" Sindomas said. "It is a delight to see you."

"Sindomas." Homar chuckled quietly. Barely a lord, he was. Sindomas had a fortress in the town of Belarrion and a standing army, but compared to his peers in Nardur he was of little consequence. "What do you want?"

"You have likely heard of Lord Elras the pretender," Sindomas said. "He has stolen the throne from the rightful heir... he has—"

For a while the petty lord's words faded from his consciousness. Lord Homar had been well aware that something had happened last night, that likely someone had entered unannounced. Lord Elras was the last person Homar would like to rule the nation, but still it was not worth all the fighting and bloodshed. It was not worth stopping the hunt. The human slave, trembling before him, was too delicious a specimen, the forest too delightful a hunting ground.

"We have made serious incursions. We would like your help. Our troops have swelled in size many times, mostly due to Lady Nar—"

"No," Homar boomed. "I will take no part in this insurrection. Be gone."

Sindomas frowned. "Ah. I thought I could count on you. You know, friend—"

"You are not my friend."

"—should we succeed you would benefit greatly."

"You will not succeed. I am certain of that."

Sindomas' face paled, and he eyed the ground. When he looked up, he no longer had the look of defeat but instead of anger. "You have erred, Homar. I have strengths you do not know. When we succeed, I will have your head."

He turned and galloped off. Homar had half a mind to chase him and cut him down. Still, he wondered if Sindomas spoke truthfully, if he had an advantage Homar knew nothing of, if he would succeed and slay Lord Elras, then come back to have Homar's head. Then he looked at his quarry—the trembling human before him and the woods behind—and he knew all that mattered for now was the hunt he loved. The war brewing in the outside world would have to wait. The human took off into the woods. He gave one last look to the stone walls of Druenel-Hai, then fixed his gaze on the fleeing prey, and all thoughts of Elras and Sindomas vanished from his mind.

~

The thrill of the hunt ended with a decisive wound and a long, satisfying bloodmeal. Once the last drop of the slave's blood had entered Homar's body, his mind once again returned to things beyond the carnal and immediate. The lord Sindomas and a woman whose name began with "Nar" were staging a rebellion, "fomenting unrest" as some would call it. To warn King Elras about it would create friendship with the new sovereign, even if it were a slight, superficial friendship. Lord Homar was not as ambitious as some, but he had read much and collected books in his personal library. If he told King Elras of what was coming, it would build trust in the decades and perhaps centuries to come in Homar's life. "Choose your friends wisely," the Lonen king, Aimon the First, wrote of his long illustrious career. "Ask yourself, 'Who is strongest?' and pledge yourself to them." The world of politics—the Great Game, as Lonen nobles called it—was a perilous business, but the wise choice was clear. Lord Elras had the upper hand. He controlled the crown jewel of Nardur, Druenel-Hai. The stone walls had stood since the first king Drusion reached age one-hundred.

In all the decades and centuries since it had not faltered, though the Andomasi raiders and treacherous lords had tried to pierce its black stone.

"Husband!"

He looked toward his wife, standing in front of Allenon Manor, their giant stone home. Samné, his third wife and the one he had loved best, had likely only just woken up, yet the slave-girls had done wondrous work: she wore her black dress and her earrings, as if she had anticipated the task before them. "Come with me, my lady," Homar said. "We shall ride to the capital together."

She looked back. "I... perhaps you should go alone, husband."

Homar glared. She was so often stubborn, like many women of noble birth. It was part of the reason Homar liked her. Even more so—he thought—as she looked down in defeat, and quickly and reluctantly headed to the stables. *Stubborn, but not too stubborn.*

Together they entered the city of Druenel-Hai. The banners of Elras—a black bat against a red field—flapped on posts at every street-corner. Besides the burnt roofs of certain homes, everything seemed the same. The Black Altar still lay in the center of the city square, an ancient relic of a forgotten time when the druen openly worshiped the Dark One. *It is good that time has passed,* he thought. The Library of Druthor remained untouched. Everything did seem as it had been, except for the people. There were fewer people here, Homar thought, or they are in hiding.

At the gate of the Black Castle, where ancient Drusion and then Druthor had ruled, two hulking guards stood by. It was impossible to tell if they were druen, but Homar had his doubts; they wielded great cleavers of swords, half their height, and disguising their faces were crabshell helmets, like those the southlanders wore.

More foreigners lurked within the winding halls of the Black Castle, whether Andomasi or Lonen it was impossible to tell.

On the Crimson Throne, Lord Elras looked more a slug than a druen. How he fit in the seat was impossible for Homar to imagine, but in truth he did not fit; much of himself, his slabs of white pasty flesh, fell out of the throne and stretched his rich silk robes to their absolute limits. In one hand he held a gilded wine-goblet, in the other a leg of lamb. Nearby him, on a table, lay what remained of his noon meal: bones licked clean of meat, half-eaten fish, bowls of sauces and dips, and several untouched bowls of Port Andom-style crab roasts, which Homar had no doubt Elras would quickly devour.

"Why do you bother me?" Elras growled and threw the half-eaten lamb leg to the ground. "I wonder why my men let you in, Homar. Your wife I don't mind... she can stay as long as she wants."

Samné audibly groaned in revulsion, and Homar did not blame her. Before Elras had turned into this glutton he had been a handsome and athletic druen, a warrior-lord who—Homar recalled—had won several battles and put down many rebellions. *How long has it been*, he wondered. *Years. Decades, perhaps.* Homar had tripled, perhaps quadrupled in size, and the thin, athletic and handsome warrior had turned into... this.

"I have come to bring word of treachery," Homar began, managing somehow to withhold his revulsion. "Lord Sindomas and others... mean to attack you. Betray you, your... Your Majesty."

Why was it so hard to say? *I am doing this for myself, not him.*

"Let them!" Elras laughed. "You know, Homar, I once thought I had a choice... food or beautiful women. But now I shall have it all. No woman in Druenel-Hai with half a mind will say no to me. Do you know how many women have been in my chambers since I became king?"

"I do not need to know." Homar couldn't help a grimace.

"You're right, and you shouldn't!" Elras squawked. "Anyway, I grow tired of you, Homar. Your wife is certainly something. I wonder why she chose you. I shall want her in my chamber tonight."

"No!" Homar snapped. "Absolutely not!"

"Have you gone mad?" Elras cackled. "You refuse your king? You know you come in uninvited to the Black Castle. By rights I could drink you dry. Your wife, and yourself. Is it preferable to you that I drink you dry, or that I have what I deserve?"

Drink us dry, he almost said, but kept quiet. The thought of Elras bedding his wife sickened him on her behalf. Homar had barely known Elras as a young lord, but he had turned from a promising warrior into this.

"We will be going," Homar intoned. "I am sorry we wasted our effort."

"You will not go!" Elras said. "My mercenaries respect me. I pay them well, better than any other master they've ever had. They'll not hesitate to do anything I command. If I told them to kill you they'd do so without a second's thought."

"You will not have my wife," Homar said, "because I will not allow it… and also because it isn't possible. How you perform in bed, wearing that giant white sack of flesh, I cannot imagine. I will defend her with my life if need be." Homar drew his sword from its sheath. "Your fat, greasy hands won't touch her. I will kill you, slug—mark my words."

"Guards!" Elras howled, and then burst into laughter. He gulped all the wine from his goblet, red liquid trickled all over his fat white cheeks, then tossed it clattering to the stone floor.

Behind him, footsteps echoed. Homar pivoted around, and the two mercenaries who had stood outside the door now approached him, halberds at the ready, faces obscured by crabshell helmets.

"Oh, Samné," Elras purred. "I have always had a fondness for you. Ever since I saw you I thought you deserved better than this peon."

Homar's wife was rigid, immobile.

"Your husband now gets what he has deserved all this time… finally the better man wins. So I ask you, Samné, of your own free will, who do you choose?"

"Quiet, slug!" Homar hissed. But his breathing had grown hoarse. His heart pounded like a drum.

"I choose my husband," Samné breathed.

The saint. If Homar were in her position, he had no idea what he would do.

"I choose you, Elras," she finished.

For a moment Homar froze, utterly stunned. Elras cackled behind him. "Very well, Queen Samné, my wife. Do not bother with divorce. Mercenaries, take care of this odious weakling."

Who should I kill, Homar thought for a second, looking first at Elras. Then he turned and charged Samné, heaving his sword above his head. As he brought it down the first puncture of the halberd split bone and tore through his chest. The sword dropped from his hand.

Elras laughed, and Samné laughed with him.

CHAPTER SIX:
MONSTER

Lunitari, Slave

Drastheon-by-the-Sea could scarcely be called a village. Besides the Manor where the crown prince lived in hiding, there was quite clearly no development. Homes lined the road, of course, but these were wattle-and-daub huts completely unlike the stone-walled, tile-roofed buildings of the capital. In a makeshift market, near the choppy ocean, teams of fishermen unloaded the morning catches—crabs, still squirming with life, and nets full of haddock—and villagers met them to purchase what would be their daily meal.

At the door of the manor, Lunitari wondered if he was making a mistake. The warriors of *dó kentas* valued their honor and duty more than their life, but Lunitari wondered what he, a Lamen—a soldier of Light and Life—had to do with this dark and violent land. But as *dó kentari* he learned to ignore the cares and worries of the mortal world. He knocked firmly on the door of the Manor and waited.

Moments passed. He knocked again, but again there was no answer. He laid his fingers round the doorknob, twisted it slightly, and it opened up. From within the Manor, the scent of musk and mildew billowed outward. Yet as he took the first tentative step, putting pressure on the loose floorboards, he could not help but notice a different smell... the smell of food.

Honor, prowess, and most pertinently, wisdom: the three strengths of *dó kentas*. He had his quarterstaff ready, ready as always, but he moved as quietly as he could manage—and not much, with these creaking floorboards.

The narrow hallway took him to a kitchen. A woman with thick salt-and-pepper hair diced onions on a board. A pink slab of rabbit meat lay nearby. Lunitari's stomach growled, though food was the last thing he should concern himself with.

"I heard you from the door!" the woman shrieked, and in an

instant spun around, holding the knife out like a weapon. She was old... older than Halé, Druthor's sixth wife. Lunitari could tell by her wrinkled face. Wrinkles did not come quickly to druen or to elves in general. And her eyes had a frantic look as she glared at Lunitari— frantic, and yet exasperated, like someone who had worked hard and received nothing in return. "Who are you? Who are you, gold-hair? Speak, or I will hurt you. I am a homebody, but I won't tolerate any intrusions."

"I have come for the crown prince."

The woman laughed joylessly. "Ah, Dorrias, that monster upstairs. He is busy picking wings off flies, probably. I managed to stop him from dissecting squirrels, but it was a great deal of effort. Effort I wish I had spent elsewhere... and Druthor will have my head if I run."

"Druthor is dead," Lunitari said. He supposed news traveled slowly this far south. "That is why I have come."

The woman cackled. "Thirty years of my life. And I am free! Free! He will be the country's problem now, not mine. Free! Free! I am free! Perhaps there are gods after all. The gods killed Druthor so I wouldn't have to deal with Dorrias! Oh, praise the gods—I thought I'd never utter such foolish words." Tears streaked her wrinkled cheeks. "Oh, gold-hair, you are probably a messenger from Heaven aren't you?"

"No."

"Oh, quiet," she growled. "The monster is your problem now. I want him out of here this instant. Go get him, gold-hair. The Manor is mine now. The monster is yours. Get him and leave. I will not want to see his horrid face anymore. I am free. Free! I am free!"

Spurred on by her words, Lunitari fled the kitchen. *There are two monsters in this house*, he thought. He had only met one.

Sure enough, in a dank upstairs attic, a druen crouched in the darkness. Though fat, his knees nearly touched his ears as he knelt, while his hands picked the wings off a fly. All around him, wingless flies buzzed in agony, unable to move except for their tiny legs. It was cruel, Lunitari thought, and remembered the Tree Folk who lived across the sea, the elves of the Umen Tribe, who dared not harm beasts. They calmed them, befriended them, and would not even kill a fly—dirty, vicious things though they were—let alone torture them, maim them, and leave them with no quality of life.

"Dorrias," Lunitari intoned.

The crown prince caught another fly, picking him by his wings, having dropped his last victim. "What do you want?" he said in a gravelly voice. "I am busy."

"I... see that..." Lunitari felt like retching, looking at the myriad wingless flies all around the crown prince, buzzing in agony. "Your father is dead. The kingship goes to you. I am only a messenger. The Crimson Throne... is yours." Lunitari bit his lip. He wondered if Dorrias was the last thing Nardur needed—no, he was certain of it—but he remembered he only did his duty. This is not my land, he reminded himself. Its proper governance does not concern me. Yet as Dorrias stood up, he wondered if it were a cruel act to foist this creature upon the citizens of Nardur, evil-hearted though they were. "Go to the capital. The kingship is yours."

"I do not know the way." Dorrias dropped another maimed fly and speared another as it buzzed by his nose. "I don't remember how to get there. I was little when I left."

"I... I will show you." Lunitari couldn't believe what he was saying. But to a disciple of *dó kentas*, honor was more important than life.

Dorrias, having removed the wings from the fly he had just caught, dropped it to the floor and then smashed it with his fingers. "First I shall get rid of all these traitors. I can hear them buzzing, conspiring against me. Flies are wicked things."

Lunitari's stomach turned. Indeed, he was foisting a madman upon the folk of Nardur. But it is not my land. It is not my fight. His only goal had been to make certain his master's will be done. It was King Druthor that was mad for deigning Dorrias heir, not Lunitari.

One by one Dorrias crushed the flies with his finger, pronouncing their crimes. "Treason!" he snapped. "Sedition! Inciting violence! Rebellion!"

Worried he would vomit, Lunitari headed downstairs to wait

for Dorrias, and gather his thoughts.

CHAPTER SEVEN:
THE SIEGE BEGINS

Sindomas of House Samsani, Lord of Belarras

The bodies lay in the fading twilight, spread out all before them. They had won against Lord Rumi, who had pledged loyalty to the false king Elras. He had made a grave mistake; now in retreat, he had no protection against what came next. Sindomas' sword had taken the lives of nine soldiers and wounded countless others. While Narité the Black Widow stood back and watched, staff in hand, Sindomas had led the charge personally, and—filled with inspiration—his soldiers had driven deep into the enemy ranks. But it had been at great cost; though Sindomas won the victory, only a hundred of his own men remained alive.

"Another victory will destroy us," Sindomas mused, and sheathed his sword.

"No," Narité laughed. "No, you are wrong, good sir." She dismounted from her palfrey and plopped onto the dirt road. She touched her staff to her breast. Then, as a green light began to grow in the black stone on its tip, she strode out slowly into the field of bodies. The air chilled and gooseflesh spread across Sindomas' skin. He had a hunch of what would come next.

One by one, the dead arose, some headless and some armless but all animate again. Even severed hands were charged with this false life and perked up at the ready, preparing to crawl along as fellow soldiers. Other felled soldiers grabbed their severed heads and held them tight to their chests. And every creature—whether wounded soldier, animate hand, or headless warrior—fixed its attention on Narité the Black Widow, their master. "Follow me, children of the night! We must march to Druenel-Hai before the sun rises."

Before dawn, they reached the capital city, its black walls

stretching high above the pines. Sindomas had brought all the siege machinery he feasibly could—two catapults, now driven by walking dead, and three ballistae operated by the few soldiers still alive.

"We must break in before daylight," Narité said. "There are limits to my power. The undead burn away in the light of the sun."

Lord Sindomas gulped. "I wish you had told me before."

"Do not worry," Narité laughed. "Worrying does not suit a man of your station."

At the gate, in the dark of the summer night, the first shots of the ballistae were loosed, splintering the ages-old South Gate. Soon after, warning-bells clanged from Nardur's many towers. A sudden assault, a breach, and they would certainly win; the walking dead, the children of the night, outnumbered the living soldiers within. A victory was possible. But death would come with the dawn.

CHAPTER EIGHT:
MIDNIGHT JOURNEY

Lunitari, Slave

The journey took them along the main roads. The night was dark, and Lunitari sensed the night was evil. Nocturnal journeyers—a thing only seen in druen lands—spoke amongst themselves of an army of the dead, summoned by a great witch of fell powers. Rumormongers whispered of betrayal and strife throughout the entire vampire nation, and the Lonely Temple where the Black Zealots once presided lying empty, unprotected from robbers. But who in their right mind would rob the citadel of the Black Zealots? Had there ever been a more foolish course of action in the history of Varda?

Lunitari gripped his staff so tight his hands grew sweaty. Behind him, he could hear Dorrias' earth-shaking trudges. Shadowy figures appeared on the road ahead. Instinctively Lunitari turned and grabbed Dorrias' pudgy hands. The crown prince snarled but Lunitari yanked him off the roadside and hissed, "Keep quiet."

Out of the gloom a group of three emerged: a vampire woman in a long black woolen robe, a book clutched in her long white fingers. A scholar, perhaps… or an antipriest, though those had not been seen in Lunitari's time. To her right strode a man in a similar black robe, and to her left a human slave. *Just a druen family on a midnight journey*. Lunitari bit his lip. The night indeed was evil; he had lost his grasp of what he should fear. *Why would anyone be looking for me? How would anyone even know who I am?*

Another half-hour passed down the road. More travelers appeared ahead, and Lunitari determined not to overreact. There were two this time—a man in red robes, and a soldier in full armor, wearing a Lonen-style crabshell helmet and bearing a halberd. Lunitari tried to pass them by, but the red-cloaked man shouted "Stop!" and Lunitari instinctively obeyed. He turned around to face him.

"Who are you?" the red-cloaked man hissed.

"I am this man's bondservant," Lunitari said. "A slave. His warrior."

"And who are you, then?" the red-cloaked man hissed, turning his feral eyes to Dorrias.

"He is mute," Lunitari said. "He cannot speak."

"I am Dorrias," he said, the idiot.

"Dorrias?" The red-cloaked man's face twisted into a wolfish grin. "Dorrias, of the Druesi family? The crown prince himself?"

"Yes."

"He is a halfwit," Lunitari snapped. "He doesn't know what he is talking about. Please, let us by."

The red-cloaked man nodded to his armored servant. In an instant, his halberd was plunged through Dorrias' chest.

Lunitari had his quarterstaff out, heart pounding out of control. *The cause is lost*, he thought, and now all he needed was vengeance. The red-cloaked vampire reached for a dagger on his belt but Lunitari struck first, striking his skull with one end of the quarterstaff. He shrieked and fell backward, off the road and into the brush. Lunitari leapt after him, slamming the tip between his eyes and breaking his nose. One last slam of the quarterstaff, fracturing his skull, and Lunitari knew he would likely never wake up.

The armored man struck with his halberd, but Lunitari knocked it aside with his quarterstaff. He had entered the state of battle, the focused union with *dó kentas*. The soldier had the strength of steel and armor, but Lunitari had the strength of the Way; he focused only on battle and martial perfection, casting all fear and worry aside, no longer hearing the beating of his heart nor sensing the exhaustion that racked his body. In total focus he cast aside each blow with his staff, striking whenever the opportunity arose but never succumbing to the worries of the flesh.

He moved in, thrust his staff behind the man's legs and pushed ahead for the trip. The soldier's armored body struck the dirt road like a bag of stones. Lunitari drew his longknife from its sheath and slipped the narrow blade between the plates of the soldier's armor. He struck without any cares for mercy. He struck until the focus of *dó kentas* faded, until the struggle of the flesh won out and he rose from his bloody deed, panting and thoroughly exhausted. His once-white robe had turned mostly red.

He had done what the code of *dó kentas* required of him— everything he could. He had tried to enact his liege's will. But it seemed justice could not be done in the nation of vampires. Once again he thought of the cynical Lonen author: "There is nothing except what lies around us, nothing except strength and weakness, wealth and poverty, a battle between the self-interests of all."

It had not seemed true in Lunitari's homeland. But it seemed true here. For now, everything was clear to him: he had done his part in the nation of the vampires. The harbor of the druen would not give safe passage to someone so obviously an outlander. Besides, he had no coin. The journey south would last months, and he might not survive it, but at least he would take solace in the fact that he had fulfilled the *dó kentari* code: do everything you can to serve your liege. But King Druthor was dead and long-forgotten, and Lunitari had failed.

He turned south down the road, heading home.

CHAPTER NINE:
THE FINAL BATTLE

Sindomas of House Samsani, Lord of Belarras

The gates gave out with a splintering crack. The living dead poured in from beyond, and Sindomas eyed the eastern horizon every few seconds, waiting for the sun to show her face and spell their doom. He did not want to charge, not among the evil dead, though Lady Narité seemed to have complete command over them. He found himself a dozen yards outside the shattered South Gate, watching and clutching the reins of his charger. Mercenaries in outlander armor fought valiantly against the dead. A disembodied hand crawled its way up to one's neck and squeezed tight, slowly but surely strangling him. Denizens of Druenel-Hai panicked; those out in the streets fled screaming into the darkness. The morbid army had a power not just of unmatched endurance; they also had the power of fear.

"In the end, fear is the greatest tool a general can wield," Sindomas recalled from a book of strategy, "both to deter opponents and keep the lesser beings in check." The author, a druen warlord, had died from an assassin's blade. But that did not make his words any less true.

I should be fighting, Sindomas thought. But he did not want to go near the living dead. The walking corpses were overcoming the mercenary soldiers, he realized. A severed limb or head only emboldened them. They were senseless and mindless, Sindomas guessed, but they never gave in to fear or pain. Their strikes and bites eventually found weaknesses. *We are winning*, Sindomas realized.

And then the sun rose.

The first shafts of sunlight glanced through the trees and a pale pink glow appeared on the horizon. The light hit the walking dead still outside the gates full-on. Unprotected by the shade of the walls and buildings, the sun's rays burned their flesh just as Narité had said. The bodies, exposed to the light, shrieked with white steam as they burned away. Sindomas turned and galloped off.

CHAPTER TEN:
TRAITORS

Samné of House Barazon, Drazzandoré

As the last traitor walked to the chopping block, Samné held back tears. It was so terribly cold. Summer had given way to autumn; already snow fell from the sky as hard as it did last spring. The time of endless night would soon fall upon the arctic. She regretted not bringing her cloak. She regretted not sitting by the fire.

"Lord Sindomas Samsani, vile traitor, do you have any last words?"

The pallid, thin druen shook his head. "No."

The executioner slammed his head onto the chopping block, then threw the black hood over his head and pitched back his giant axe. A clean cut was afforded to only the nobles and the friends of the king. The lowly born would suffer far more.

The axe split halfway down his neck. Samné looked away. Her husband watched as well, beside her on his cart. His giant white hands went toward her breasts.

She shivered. She regretted not bringing warmer clothing. She wept because of the cold.

THE ECSTASY

Drasanthi Giltharion, Black Zealot

Master Drudar had summoned all the Black Zealots outside the black walls of Druenel-Hai. Now, with a fire blazing in the midst of the swirling snow, the Black Zealots once more began their *ecstasy*. Hands joined they shifted shapes. "Shall we honor the new king's ascension?" Master Drudar asked as the Wolf Man. "Shall we call his reign true?"

"Yes!" Drasanthi gargled as the Skinned Witch, and all around the fire, zealots shouted the same.

~

Bells rang out all through the city of Druenel-Hai. A new king sat upon the Crimson Throne, and his reign—his sycophants proclaimed—would have no end. King Elras and Queen Samné ruled over all Nardur; but in the nation of vampires, there are no heroes, only villains, and it is anyone's guess how long they would.

PRINCE OF DREAD

Less than a decade after Elras took the throne, his own body gave out, falling victim to years and years of Andomasi crab roasts, crisp honeywine, and venison dumplings. One night in midsummer, while reclining with his wife Samné, his heart was seized by a virulent tremor, and within minutes he had fallen dead. In the wake of his passing came Homar son of Homar, Lord of Agnon, of the House of Allenon, and his reign began with his mother's death. Her meal was not poisoned; let the suspicious be ashamed, for no man of Homar's mettle would so dishonor his family.

—from the writings of Samon Druthas, Grand Historian

CHAPTER ONE:
SLAVE CATCHERS

Malirias had no name or family to speak of, no holdings or land to call his own, no home, no wife, no children… nothing, really, except his freedom and his weapons—the only two things he ever wanted.

I call no man master, he thought as he stared from his high perch onto the whitecaps. But nonetheless he drew near his destination, the port where he'd disembark—mercenary that he was—to invade the city of Dundari under the pay of King Homar, all to make amends for some long-forgotten transgression, which only the historians of the druen race remembered. It was a useless expense of the nation's resources—to level a town that bore no threat nor real enmity except in the forgotten past, all to sate the erudite King Homar's history-fueled anger—but Malirias did not care one way or the other. Only one thing mattered in life: gold, for with gold you can buy everything—women, wine, all the sensual cravings of the palate—and whoever said gold cannot buy friends lied. When Malirias had money, everyone wanted to be his friend.

He wielded his weapons—a sword and longknife—with such legendary grace and finesse that every mercenary company wanted him. But he made sure that his employer always treated him as an equal, for he had taken great precautions to remove himself the life of slavery. He had changed his name to Malirias, left his mother and father and siblings—all slaves—and become a wholly new person. Now he was no longer Dralynthi the peasant slave, but Malirias, the free swordsman who diced his foes to pieces and commanded the highest price of any warrior in the land.

It is amazing how people treat you differently when they think you are free. Just years ago he had been scum; now, he was the apple of every scheming politician and warmongering lord's eye. The price he would exact from this unnecessary war would sustain him for a decade, at least, if—as was likely the case—he did not spend it all in a few days. Gold slipped fast through his fingers, and it took a lot of blood to replenish it.

Beyond a dense thicket, the Black River opened up, snaking its way through the undergrowth before bleeding suddenly out into the North Sea. The two-dozen buildings of the port had a ramshackle defensive wall, but in recent times no one had bothered with upkeep; Homar son of Homar had all his lords in absolute control and no one dared raise a sword against him. Thus, the port was his, and it seemed it always would be his.

Out of the doors of *The Moonlight Tavern,* a bard sang the latest Lonen ballad, perhaps newly written and doubtlessly gleaned from Port Andom, the only place where things from the outside world came in contact with the world of the druen.

In the small natural harbor, a dozen ships, having dropped their anchors, waited like an army of the sea. The sun had peaked in its journey, and about a hundred druen men—warriors, judging by their scale armor and weapons of steel—stood amid the narrow streets, some talking, some waiting silently for further orders.

Then, a name: "Dralynthi—"

Malirias recoiled at it, but nonetheless pressed ahead, merging into the crowd. Dralynthi—Night-Song—was one of the most common names. Malirias had no real reason to fear. But still, every time he heard that name, he shuddered, and wondered if the game was up, and he'd be flayed alive or worse for fleeing the slave pens. *But it is only a name,* Malirias told himself.

And by the night's end, the sound of the lute and the bard's voice faded away like vapor, replaced with the sound of tossing waves and ocean froth, and the feel of cold, spraying mist on his face. Now, like he had been so many times before, he stood on the prow of the ship, heading fast out to sea.

~

"Malirias!" A gruff voice startled him at the prow. He turned and there, in the darkness of the North Sea night, was his old friend

Samari. The aging druen had sparse wisps of gray hair on his head, and a disfiguring scar across his face that Malirias, and no doubt many others, envied. Malirias and Samari had fought side-by-side in the first and ill-fated Siege of Druenel-Hai when Homar son of Homar first tried to avenge his father. But his goal—killing Lord Elras, and capturing the mother who had betrayed her family—had remained unmet, for the fortifications of Druenel-Hai remained strong, and for all Elras' eccentricities he had stowed away ample food in case of a siege.

Homar son of Homar had gone on to win battle after battle—slowly draining Elras' resources, sinking him slower and slower into debt and financial ruin—but in the end the greatest enemy of Lord Elras was his appetite and his failing heart. "It is good to see you, Samari," Malirias answered, and he meant it. Through all the battles he'd fought he would never forget the first siege of Druenel-Hai—ill-fated though it was—and more-so the warrior who had fought by his side with unflinching bravery and loyalty. Malirias was the better fighter, but Samari by anyone's estimation was the better man.

"There is talk," Samari said. "A man spoke of an escaped slave... name of Dralynthi."

Malirias felt himself go white.

"They told me a bit about him... I worry..."

"Don't tell anyone," Malirias breathed. "I beg of you, by Drusion, by Druthor, by the bloody Dark One, I beg of you do not tell anyone. I can't go back to that life... I'd rather die..."

Confusion touched Samari's eyes, and then turned to shock. "I didn't think... I... of course not, Malirias. You don't think I would ever let you down."

Malirias shook his head. He peered into the old mercenary's eyes. Memories flashed back, of the siege of Druenel-Hai, of the ladders on the wall, of he and Samari fighting together, as one. Of Malirias, sword in one hand and short blade in the other, cursing Elras' men. "Faithless! Oathbreaker!" And Samari charging in, frightening them into submission at the end of his giant crescent-moon axe.

Below decks, Malirias and the other men rolled dice, betting on piles of copper or trinkets. It was how they spent their time. Malirias, though, preferred to practice when he had the chance—or better, fight a battle in truth. Malirias was not a man of luck or chance. There was no value, no worth, in winning a game of chance. There was nothing to be proud of. Still, Malirias took his place at one of the narrow benches, as the ship tossed this way and that, scattering the piles of copper and brass one way, then another as it plowed through the ocean waves.

At some point in the night, Samari took a seat beside him and made his rounds at the dice. He had brought his own: three six-sided dies, cubes of gold that many around the table eyed throughout the night. By all accounts, Samari had done well for himself as a mercenary.

Others tossed their own die, of ebony or stone or human bone, but Samari's alone was gold, affixed with gemstones—red, green, and blue—staring at Malirias like eyes when they clattered across the table. In all, it was a wonder no one snatched them right then and there. But Malirias sat there in the dank darkness of the ship as it rocked to and fro, and focused his ears, trying hard to listen in on what they had to say. Some came from the northern hinterlands, on the edge of the Ever-Ice, where only a few scattered hamlets lay in sight of the white wasteland. Others came from Druenel-Hai, some poor and some middling. All were free. In druen lands, a slave was not used for war. War meant spoils, and spoils meant wealth; and no master wanted his slave with even a smidgeon of power. How his father and mother had come to ruin, Malirias could not say; but even his parents had become a memory, likely still toiling in the mines, tending to the master's bees, or hauling stone from the quarries, if they were not already dead. Still, the memories had been seared in his mind and he would never forget.

"Dralynthi," another trace whisper echoed through the narrow hull. In the corner, a tall druen with a long serrated saber chatted with another, slightly shorter, but clearly important judging by the rich brocade cloak and the fine steel poniard dangling from his hilt. The dim light of the candles cast a twinkling light onto its gold pommel.

Dralynthi—no, Malirias—looked down to avoid their suspicious gazes, and shut his eyes. But when he shut them, images came to him clear as day; of their lord master, culling off the sick and disabled that had become useless to him and crucifying the ones who said they couldn't work. Of the master's lieutenant, rubbing salt into the wounds of his little brother after he begged for a reprieve. Dralynthi's leg-bones became tight and cold, and his thighs tensed to stone-like hardness. A cold clammy sweat formed over the back of his neck, and his hands grew wet with sweat. All telltale signs of guilt, and the more nervous he became the more obvious it would become. *No*, he told himself. *No, they have no reason to suspect me.*

"Hail!"

The voice from behind made him half-leap up from his seat. *What a fool I am.* Behind him stood no one of import, just a common mercenary greeting his brother-in-arms. *What luck to be born free.* Malirias drew in long cold breaths. Samari was looking up at him like he'd gone mad. In the corner, the two higher-ups were staring at him, their dark eyes full of suspicion. Malirias jerked back down into his seat. Gooseflesh had spread all over his body, and each breath exerted twice the effort it normally did. Samari laid a hand on his.

"Dark One's eyes, you're wet as the sea. Calm down, friend."

But there would be no calming down. Malirias had outwitted them for many years, pretending to be someone he was not. Now, at last, his deceit would be uncovered. The punishment for an escaped slave was flaying. The skin would be ripped from his body and then, salt would be poured onto the wound. At the thought a bit of vomit swelled up to his throat, and he became dizzy and nauseous. *Perhaps*, he thought, *it would be best to fling myself off the boat, and die a sailor's death.* He had heard a death at sea was the most calm and serene way to end your life, but how would anyone know? Then again, nothing would be worse than flaying… except, perhaps, a life of slavery again, toiling under their master with no hope of escape.

"*Dark One's eyes*," Samari hissed. "I said calm down. Calm down, Malirias. Take deep breaths. Focus on the game."

The two higher-ups had once again begun talking amongst themselves. Perhaps they had lost their focus on him. *Perhaps Samari is right.* Words were good and well, but perhaps Malirias only needed a drink.

Outside, on the deck of the ship, Malirias braced himself

against the pelting rain and howling wind with a stein of bitter ale in his hand. It was little comfort. The night was dark, and the moon—a pale mistress obscured through light gray fog—reflected against the rough waters of the North Sea. Here the crab-fishermen plied a dangerous trade, searching for the favorite food of the druen, and reaped the benefits in large sums of silver and gold. Trade was permitted to the free, but not the slave. *How would my life be* different, if I were born free? Perhaps he'd be a crab-fisherman. *Perhaps...*

"Sir!" a voice called out from behind.

When Malirias turned, the same tall, pale druen from before stared at him, accompanied by his short companion.

"What is your name?"

"Dr—Drassanias." *I have lost my mind.* Chills ripped across his flesh; he went cold, his breathing growing slow and labored.

"Drassanias," the tall, pale druen said. "I am sent by a friend of King Homar Allenon... I am an investigator for the Ministry of Escaped Slaves. I am looking for someone who goes by the name Dralynthi."

"Curious," the short druen continued, "that the men around here call you Malirias. Have you changed your name? If so, why? It is enough to draw suspicion."

"I misspoke," Malirias said.

"Would you care for a quick examination?" the short druen went on. "We will take you to our quarters and you will remove your underclothes."

"I—Yes. Yes, of course!" Malirias, had done all he could to remove the brand across his chest, which his master had burned into his skin at an early age. Most times a bit of pale jelly, smeared over the mark, prevented a careless person's notice, but he did not have any on hand, and besides, these men would be thorough. There was only one thing he could hope to do, the riskiest of all ventures, but anything was worth trying, if it meant avoiding slavery and returning to the life he once had.

"What are your names?" Malirias said as he undid the rope-belt that held up his breeches. They hit the floor around his ankles.

"That is not your concern, Drassanias," the tall druen said.

"I am Little Omagon and he is Big Omagon," the short druen answered. "We work for the same woman, and have the same name."

"What are the chances?" Big Omagon added.

"Probably quite high," Malirias said, and reached down, putting his fingers around his shirt as if he meant to peel it off, but then reached for his belt and drew his sword.

Big Omagon was headless before Little Omagon screamed. Little Omagon had barely opened his mouth before another slice of the blade took his own head off at the neck. Blood instantly began to pool around them, and Malirias—grabbing some blankets from their beds—began the onerous work of cleaning up. He would be found out, certainly; it was only a matter of time.

It seemed Malirias had barely shut his eyes for a restless night of sleep when shouting broke out, of murder, "*Murder!*" on the ship. He had thought his door-jamming skills had served him well, but it was not.

Soon after, roused from the cramped corner where he had begun to drift off, the captain came rushing into the troops' quarters. "Murder does not happen on the Sea Queen. The murder of the king's agents, less so. Never! One of you will hang for this, after you're flayed in the midst of Druenel-Hai. And I think I know who. Malirias, you were the last person I saw with those two. I have no doubts you're who murdered them. So why? Why, Malirias, would you throw your life away?"

Malirias took a step back. "It wasn't me. I assure you, captain."

The captain's expression darkened. "I don't think the judge will believe that. But first, tell me why."

In the distance, Samari regarded him pityingly.

"I assure you, it wasn't me. I spoke with them only a few moments and left... you must understand, captain. Please, you must hear me out. I am the best warrior here—" He half-bit his lips at the glares; a bad tactical choice, but he had made blunders all throughout this trip. He had spoken himself into so many situations, he might as well have stabbed his sword and longknife into himself; and in truth that became a better and better option each minute. *Death is better than slavery.* "I beg of you," he went on. "You have no evidence."

"Evidence," the captain grunted. "No, perhaps I do not. Perhaps, Malirias, if you do not confess, I will kill a friend of yours—"

"Captain, Malirias is an escaped slave." Of all the voices below decks, he least expected Samari. "His true name is Dralynthi, and when the king's agents found out he must have killed them."

"Bastard. Mongrel. Son of a whore," Malirias mumbled.

The captain's face lit up with sharkish delight. Wry, sadistic smiles touched the crewmates' lips. Samari's face was expressionless. "You will not receive good treatment, Malirias, when the king's men hear of this. Ah, I wish I could watch what they decide to do to you."

"Sir." The water of the North Sea was ice-cold; a jump in, and the shock would make you instantly begin to drown. *What to do, what to do?* Malirias found himself edging toward the door. He found his hands grasping the hilt of his longknife and longsword. He thought he might run. Perhaps, he could overcome all these mercenaries. Perhaps, if he was the best fighter among them, he could overcome all these hundred soldiers. Perhaps...

"Lower your weapons, Dralynthi," the captain said, the sharkish smile growing across his face. "If you know what is best for you, you will surrender." He drew a weapon of his own, a long curved saber of southern make.

"Sir," Malirias repeated, silently weighing options in his mind, though he knew there was only one: death.

"I will count down from five. Five... four..."

A few yards separated them from each other.

"Three... two..."

Malirias leapt the distance and sliced with his sword, which whistled in the air. The captain just barely caught it with his southern curve blade, but Malirias answered with a firm stab into the chest with his longknife. He twisted it underneath him and the captain gargled. In that instant, chaos broke loose. A mercenary came running at him with a huge axe, intending to bludgeon and bloody him, but Malirias stepped under him and hacked down hard, popping off his arm at the shoulder. Then he barreled for the doorway and sprinted above decks. A few sailors shouted commands at each other; the winds had picked up, and though the sun had begun to glow above the sea, turning the clouds red and pink, it was still terribly difficult to see. *If I will die*, Malirias decided, so, too, *will all these others. I will let the sea take care of them*. He dashed for the first sailor he saw, totally unprepared for the heavy slice he dealt him, cleaving his neck in twain like a chopped carrot. His head hit the floor and his body began to bleed out. An arrow zipped out at him, grazing his neck; it hit the wooden railing with a thud. A mercenary stood in the distance, bow in hand.

Samari stood there, crescent-moon axe in hand. "Stop!" he called out. "Stop this madness!"

Malirias had half a mind to bolt across the deck and kill the friend he trusted, the one who betrayed him. The sailors fled in a panic. Malirias chased them down. Two were dead; two remained, screaming as they ran. Malirias bolted across the deck as mercenaries poured out of the hull. One, he stabbed in the back. Another shouted "Dark One's eyes!" as Malirias grabbed his shoulder, then ran the blade of his longknife across his neck.

Malirias gasped and took a stiff step backward. When he looked down, the goosefeather fletching of an arrow stuck out of his chest, near his heart. Another arrow struck him, hard, and he fell to the cold wet deck. He was dying. *But at least I will die free.*

CHAPTER TWO:
FORGOTTEN LAND

Samari could scarcely think after what had happened. A senseless loss of life, certainly, and one he wished he could have avoided. He did not, in truth, know whom to blame more: the runaway slave who had killed all the knowledgeable sailors, or the slave-catchers who had driven him into the suicidal massacre. In the end, it did not matter who he blamed. Samari and the hundred-fifty or so other mercenaries were alone at sea, with no other ships in sight and no hopes of going home. The winds had picked up, and by any account it seemed a storm was headed their way.

A few mercs began to shout in a panic. There was no land in sight, but at least they knew that the land was west, the direct opposite of the sun; beyond, to the east, was only water and, according to legend, the world's end, where the ocean bled out into a great waterfall. And below, who knew what awaited a sailor who had fallen off the world? The fires of damnation, or the elysium of paradise, like the do-gooders claimed awaited the dead? There was no way of knowing; no sailor had ever made it to the edge of the world, for though some had tried, it was simply too far.

"Calm down! Calm yourselves!" Samari hissed. "Do any of you know how to operate these sails? Be calm, and answer!"

"Wouldn't one of us have said so if we did?" snarled a man he recognized as Gilthari, an archer from Belarras, and possibly the one who had stricken Malirias dead. "We are going to die out here! At least we have this oaf to patronize us!"

"You're acting a coward," Samari intoned. "I would quiet down. Besides—"

"Look!" shouted a young merc Samari didn't recognize. "Land!"

Across the growing waves of the sea, the pink sunlight illuminated a set of high brown hills and a rocky beach. The winds and the waves were blowing them toward it.

"Get ready. I suspect we will not have an easy landing."

"Thanks, Ma," Gilthari sneered.

Samari shook his head.

~

With a wood-splitting groan, the ship drove into the rock pebbles of the beach. A few mercs lost their footing and skidded across the deck, and one just barely avoided splashing into the water by clutching the railing. Together, they poured out, leaping onto the froth-covered rocks. Black birds circled overhead, cawing even as thunderheads appeared over the west.

Samari wondered where they were. They had been little more than a day out to sea. They could not be too far out of Nardur, though he supposed it was possible. All around them were high, near-mountainous brown hills. Besides the black birds—now gone to hide from the storm—and the crass shouts and curses of the mercs, there was nothing; only an empty land of high, brown-grassed hills, blown about by strong buffeting winds. To reach Port Andom and meet up with the other ships, they'd have to head south down the coast for dozens, perhaps a hundred miles. They would already be far too late. The more practical proposition—returning to Nardur and Druenel-Hai—nonetheless had great risks and dangers. Defectors, in the law's eyes, were little better than escaped slaves. They had not truly defected, of course, but judges had no leniency, and the folk of Nardur enjoyed a good execution better than a good song or a brilliant play.

Like a mob, Samari and the other mercs ambled down the high hills and the wave-washed pebbles where crabs eked out their joyless existences. Within the hour, it began to rain. A spear of lightning and a crack of thunder heralded the coming storm.

~

The rain turned the hills—when they had to cross them—muddy and slippery. It was not long before noon when they decided to give up for the day and wait out the storm. But they had no tent, nor any means of making a fire, and so—in spite of the gloominess of the day and the cracking lightning and thunder—Samari and the mercs could at last bear it no longer, and again headed south down the coast through the miserable rain.

A headache overtook all Samari's thoughts; his nose began to drip yellow and burn at the slightest touch. This mud, rain, and chill weather was the perfect condition for sickness and malaise to grow. But eventually the rain eased and the sun—now firmly in the west—sank beneath the brown muddy hills, once again becoming a pale glow. The storm stopped not long after; the rain faded to nothing, and night set in.

"All because of Malirias," growled Gilthari. "This is all because of him. I should have stuck him with my dagger while I had the chance. I would have liked to see him flayed. I wasted an arrow on him, gods damn it. No, two! Two good arrows, on a lying, cheating, whore-son escaped slave!"

"Calm down," Samari said, eyeing the silent hills. "Why don't we just keep quiet and have our rest... let the sea soothe us to sleep?"

Gilthari sneered. "Don't try to coddle us, Samari."

"I'm not trying to," Samari breathed. The last bit of light still lit up the sky, turning the hills to black silhouettes. Behind him, the waves washed through the rocks steadily. The sound of the surf reassured him, taking away a goodly bit of his deep-seated unease. The caw of the crows returned; the black shapes circled above-head, perhaps wanting the dry biscuits and trail rations they'd salvaged from the ship. Samari laid on the driest patch of ground he could find, with his feet touching the water-washed pebbles. He set the head of his crescent-moon axe across his chest, and shut his eyes. Sleep did not come to him for a long while. He listened instead to the mercs' conversations, those that did not decide to sleep.

"Port Andom is far," one said. "We might be walking for days. Weeks, maybe."

"Quiet, Ras," another answered. "Don't give me a worse headache than I need."

"There would have been women in Port Andom," Ras answered. "Beautiful, brown-haired Andomasi women..."

"There still will be."

"If we aren't dead."

Chills touched Samari's neck.

"Why would we be dead?" Ras's friend answered.

"There are wolves outside Port Andom. Big wolves, fierce wolves. Worse than those in Nardur…"

"Quiet," Ras's friend said. "You're scaring me."

But for some reason, wolves were the last thing he was afraid of.

~

Samari woke in the dark before the morning, when the air was sweet with the possibilities of the coming day. Though, he mused, there would be nothing good or great that came with the sun's light, only emptiness and the promise of more hiking, more torturous days to come. There was rustling, a few brushes of metal pots, someone walking through the muddy grass. Perhaps the merc who'd been stuck with watch duty. Samari gave a passing glance around, then lay down again on the bed of moist grass.

More clattering echoed through the air, the sounds of someone talking or groaning in their sleep. Samari again shut his eyes and drifted off.

~

Shouts awoke Samari when the sky had brightened to white. He scrambled to his feet, axe in hand. A crowd of mercs hovered over the body of a druen, lifeless and drained of blood. Two bite-marks pocked his neck.

"What is the meaning of this?" Samari rushed up to them. "Who did this? Who was on watch?"

"This is Drusari, and he was on watch," Gilthari's voice spoke above the others. "At least, I thought he was. If he had been, he'd not be dead."

"I heard him snoring," said another merc. "A bad watchman,

he was."

"Apparently some among us think it's all okay to drink the blood of your fellow druen," Gilthari sneered. "The paramount grievance against justice and order and the law of Nardur."

"No," Samari found himself saying. "I awoke in the early morning hours, and I heard someone walking around. I thought it was the man on watch…"

"You awoke in the early morning hours, when Drusari was drunk dry?"

Samari snarled at Gilthari's accusation. "Don't be ridiculous. I'd guess my sense of honor is far greater than yours."

Gilthari looked down, apparently ready to drop the thought before it had begun. "So whom?"

Samari eyed the hills. "Perhaps… we are not alone."

Gilthari's eyes narrowed. "Ah, yes, I'm certain. A spook or a gremlin is always the most logical assertion."

"No… the lost tribe," someone said—a druen of average height, hair bound in a ponytail and dressed in a jerkin of boiled leather, a bow in hand—whose voice he recognized as Ras. "The offspring of Sarsoli, child of Gilden. Some say they live beyond the land of Nardur, in the hill country…"

"Quiet," Gilthari snapped. "I won't hear any more talk of this idiocy. We head south at once. We don't stop until nightfall. We will make it to Port Andom if we stop telling fanciful tales to scare each other and actually march. Now, come on."

They began their march once more, down the pebble-strewn beaches in the shadow of the high hills. Samari could no longer deny the nervousness growing in the pit of his stomach, nor the sudden movements and jerks when the shadow of a bird passed over them. He had never heard of the Lost Tribe before, but surely it made sense. The ancient patriarch of the druen, Prince Gilden, had a very messy family life if the history-books were to be believed. Samari was not a reading man, but scholars had told him that Sarsoli disappeared somewhere along the voyage north. Why would it not make sense that he had come here, to these barren empty hills, and built a life for himself among his depraved offspring?

The beach continued its sloping, ambling path. By the time the sun dipped low on the second day, the end of these hills was in sight; beyond lay a grassy plain with scattered thickets of pines, a few hundred yards away. But Samari and the mercs had grown exhausted, and rest was far too tempting by the time the sky had grown completely dark.

Feet aching with the stress of the march, Samari sat down and removed his boots, whose soles he had worn to near-tatters. The stench followed but the other soldiers were already asleep or near it. The sky—gone completely dark—offered very little light, but Samari could see the man they'd appointed for the first watch was reclining against one of the hills and it was quite likely, in a period of time, that he would neglect his duties.

Fighting off his own sleepiness, Samari massaged his aching, sore feet. He praised the spirits everyone had fallen asleep, for the stench was about as bad as could be expected.

By the time he'd again put on his worn-down boots, the watchman reclining against the hill had fallen into a snoring heavy sleep. *I guess it is me who will serve as first watch.* To waken himself, he stood up and decided to go for a walk in the chill night air. Through a maze of sleeping druen, he stepped through the camp like eggshells and ascended the first of the mountainous hills.

Crescent-moon axe in hand, Samari walked through the silence of the night and reflected on all that had gone on. Malirias had been his friend, but in the end Samari's sense of duty had overcome him. As a young man, Samari had served in the present king's wars against Elras, the one he called "the pretender." In mind and body, Homar son of Homar was twice, perhaps thrice the man Elras was. He had stolen practically the entire kingdom from the slug; the war was won by the time Elras' body succumbed to a life of sweet-rolls, sweet-cakes, mead, and Andomasi crab roasts. And as a close confidante of King Homar, he knew the truth of all that had gone on. Homar had been a teen when his mother joined with Lord Elras, and—at the end of his ascension—Homar had committed what many called the ultimate crime. His mother, Samné, by now had become a shadow of what she once had been; old and weak, with more gray hairs than black, a pitiful woman who had all but given up on life. Yet even in her wretched state, Homar's wrath could not be quelled. Homar had gone to the best apothecary in Druenel-Hai, and ordered a virulent poison of Wildman's Beard extract, and Samari had been there when Homar added it to his mother's mead. A weak wretch by now, she had taken the chalice and said she was not thirsty or hungry.

"Drink it," Homar had demanded of her.

And his mother had refused again, saying she was not thirsty.

Then Homar had forced it to her lips and said, "Only the best for my sweet, loving mother."

Homar had to force it down her mouth before she finally swallowed. He had watched her as she bled through her mouth and slowly died, but even her death could not cure the hurt. Some wounds never heal, and vengeance—if a person exacts it themselves—rarely assuages deep injuries. Samari sometimes thought Homar had regretted the killing, though he'd never admit it. It was justice, perhaps, but Homar son of Homar would never forget the ruin that had fallen on his family.

The dark of the night—in the midst of the silence of the hills—had made it so easy to reminisce about the past. Some things stay with you forever, and Samari would never forget his liege's ascension to the Crimson Throne.

Panting, by now, Samari turned back toward the sound of the rushing waves. The clouds had broken away, revealing the moon and stars, painting the North Sea with their bright pinpoints of light. Below, where the mercs were sleeping, strangers had come into the camp and shouting, in an instant, broke the long silence.

Perched safe at the top of the hill, Samari weighed his best option. Dozens of thin, pale-white and naked druen swarmed the camp, and the mercs were severely unready. A few of these gangly creatures had already found their victims, laying in with their fangs and drinking them dry.

"WAGH!" one screamed, jolting Samari. He whipped around and saw another of these bony, deformed creatures running toward him from the darkness. He struck hard with his crescent-moon axe; the steel bit took it in the forehead, splitting clean through its skull and sending chunks of brain into the air. Samari's heart erupted into an out-of-control pounding. He had little time to decide. In all, blind with fear and self-preservation, he bolted away from the camp, the scene of the massacre, toward the plain south of the hills.

Screams from mercenaries and more shrieks of ecstasy from these mutant druen only spurred him to run faster. In the end, he and Ras had been right; there were people in these hills. Perhaps, Sarsoli had indeed come here, and these—these things—were his inbred mutant descendants.

"WAGH!" another wild druen screamed. "TEAR FLESH FROM BONES!"

"WAGH!" another screeched. "BLOOD! WAGH! BLOOD!"

But soon the noise and terror of the ambushed camp was far behind him and Samari was running for his life, sprinting as fast as he possibly could toward the plains, worrying at every turn that these mutants would follow him there and drink him dry.

CHAPTER THREE:
THE GREAT EXPANSE

Samari headed south from the monstrous hills, walking until well after daybreak. The light of the rising sun illuminated the gloomy landscape all around him: stands of shrub-pine, tall brown grass that—by the looks of it—no one had trod for years. He couldn't shake the trembling in his fingers, the constant near-slipping of his crescent-moon axe. He would never forget the monstrous things that attacked him, the druen gone mad. He prayed to the gods he'd never see the likes of them ever again. And he had abandoned his men.

Not in a hundred years had he ever thought he'd be a deserter. There were few things he'd less rather be. *But I am alive*, he consoled himself, *while they are not.* It was small comfort. He wandered the wilderness, now, as little more than a refugee. When—and if—he made it to the city of Dundari, no one would need to know he had deserted his men. But it was quite possible he'd never make it at all… summers were short in the north, and by the end of the week it might well begin to snow. And for that, he was ill-prepared.

~

The day blended together; Samari grew to know the tall brown grass and thick, dark-needled pines, and the ominous silence of the white cloudy sky. By the time twilight came, he had come to a dark-pebbled beach, and beyond lay the salt waters of the North Sea. He could not see the other side. But he was ravenously hungry.

He continued in the twilight, growing hungrier and hungrier as the sky began to darken. He thanked the sun for long summer days. In the end he kept walking, trying to ignore his growling stomach and the weakness that hunger caused. Some time as the sun was casting its last throes of light, a thorny bush full of bright red berries appeared, and he dashed over to it as fast he could. He plucked every last berry from the bush and ate them all as the rain began to pour. Under the meager

shade of a pine tree, Samari nonetheless went to sleep hungry…
hungry, wet, and cold.

~

It was still raining when the day's first light awoke him. He was
still tired, and his stomach churned as he stood to his feet. Within
seconds, he was keeled over, vomiting, and he quickly undid his belt as
he relieved himself on the other end. *Curse me for eating those berries. Curse
me. And curse that rain.*

Though sick, he kept on, not sure where to go. In the end he
decided to go west; for to the east was the open sea, and he could not
swim his way to Dundari.

The rain only made things more miserable. Every half hour,
Samari had to keel over and vomit. And with each vomit, he became
hungrier. He could never remember being quite this miserable. He was
quite clearly in the middle of nowhere; no one lived here, and, in all, he
knew he should go back to Nardur; but even in this horrid state, in the
cold pelting rain and the constant nausea, he knew what the king's
justices would do to him: execution in the midst of Druenel-Hai.

By the end of the second day he'd gone near mad with hunger,
and it seemed there were no animals in this wilderness, or perhaps they
were afraid of him. Eventually, the rain stopped, and he fell asleep on
the damp grass.

It was dark when he awoke to a howl. Wolves. He leapt to his
feet, a hand on his crescent-moon axe, and for a moment he was less
worried about hunger and more about his own safety. The clouds had
all passed away, baring the starlit glory of the night and the moon—
now full, a pale mistress casting eerie light on the tall grass—hanging
overhead. He had half a mind to swim across the ice-cold waters just
south of where he stood, but he had no idea how wide the waters were.
Instead, axe in hand, he began to walk around it. The night had grown

cold, so cold it reminded him that winter was coming.

A wolf howled again, closer. Two more answered. *They know there is a feast here.* But Samari would not run; he could never outrun a wolf, and fear attracted them. It would be best to stay calm.

The moonlight gleamed against silver fur. A low angry growling filled the night. More silver fur appeared; the growling became a chorus. He counted eight. They had him cornered, and they were ready to make a move. Samari took his axe in both hands, and in an instant a wolf darted at him. The curved bit split its canine skull, and it whimpered. Another darted at him and he took it in the mouth with a hard side-swing. Another came right as he swung, and clamped his left leg in its teeth, then dragged him to the ground. Another wolf came running for his throat; he dropped his crescent-moon axe and grabbed the beast by the neck. Samari sank his own fangs into the wolf's neck and began to drink.

The blood took his mind to elysian heights, filling him with ecstasy and boundless energy. A few seconds into the bloodmeal, all hunger vanished from him, replaced with bottomless strength. Thirty seconds later, when all the wolf's blood had gone into his stomach and veins, he realized the wolf had nearly shredded his calf. With a cry of pain he wrenched it free. Weakly he stood up, once again grabbing his axe. The moonlight glinted over more patches of silver fur; there were thirteen wolves now, not including the two dead; and more were emerging out of the dim night. He was surrounded. There was only one option: to swim.

~

Powered by the blood meal, though hampered by the wounded leg and the weight of the axe (now strapped to his back), he swam for indeterminate time. At some point, totally exhausted and sure he would drown—the warmth of his bloodmeal the only thing preventing the icy grip of the North Sea—his leg brushed against the ground, and he stood up in the shallow water. He walked only a few moments before he collapsed onto the dry ground in a deep sleep.

~

The sun did not warm him; it had little power, this far north, even in the summer. But eventually he woke up in the light, seeing a leg bitten and thrashed by a wolf's teeth, bloody and flaring with pain at the slightest touch. *At least*, he thought, *I am not hungry.* But beyond where he lay sprawled and injured, all he could see were rolling hills, knee-high grass, and occasional pine-thickets. *The Great North Plain,* he realized. By horse, Dundari was a week distant; and that was if he knew the way, and if winter weren't coming. Soon the plain would become slick with ice and blinded with snow. And in this state, Samari would die. *I will die here*, he realized. *But at least I am no longer hungry.*

He tried to sit up, but the leg flared with incalculable pain. He could no longer walk. So he began to crawl. By noon, he collapsed, arms flaring with effort.

At night, he awoke again to a drizzling rain. Birds circled overhead. He fell back asleep.

By morning, he again was ravenously hungry. But if he remained where he was, he would die. Using the crescent-moon axe as leverage, and with indescribable pain, he pulled himself to his feet, and began to hobble across the plain, using his axe as a makeshift walking-stick. Each step sent spasms of pain through his entire body, and tears of pain welled in his eyes, but he kept walking all day until the dark of night. The grassy plain and its gently-rolling hills continued, mostly featureless and empty, and as the days bled into each other the weather slowly cooled.

Starving, weak, and barely healed, Samari had lost track of the days by the time the first snow fell. He might well have been walking for a month, for all he remembered, though he knew if that were true the first blizzard would have come. Nonetheless, the first snowflakes had begun to fall, and his tattered, rain-soiled cloak did little to protect him from the elements. Still the plain rolled on, with no hope of ending; the gnawing hunger had near consumed him, and he had tried to eat the grass numerous times, only to spit it out. He had begun to feast on whatever insects he could find, but they only made him hungrier.

Snow-flurries increased; the chill sapped what little vestiges of strength remained. Days and nights bled into each other. His body was ready to give out when a broad dirt road appeared. He wondered where it led. He fell asleep at its side, though it was morning.

CHAPTER FOUR:
A TOWN BESIEGED

An hour into his sleep, a foot nudged him awake. He was so hungry and weak he wanted to snap at whoever it was. A person, he realized, an elven man, wearing the flame-gold robes of a Healer. His gold hair, tied into a ponytail, made it clear he was not a druen at all.

"Where am I?" Samari groaned.

"You are wounded," the Healer answered in a dialect most certainly non-druenic. "I can mend them for a small donation to the Temple of Light."

Samari groaned again at the man's words. "Where am I?" he repeated.

"I see you are one of them."

"One of whom?"

The Healer's blue eyes held a mixture of compassion and distrust. In his right hand, he clutched a staff mounted with a white crystal orb. "The sons of Gilden. Your kin lay siege to the King's outpost. It is no matter; I will heal you, druen, if you promise not to join your wild brethren."

With all the strength Samari had left, he forced himself to his feet, so that he stood eye-level with the healer. "I know what will heal me," Samari said, and prepared to leap upon him, drink all the worthless blood from his veins. He had barely jerked forward an inch before the Healer's staff struck him in the forehead, stunning him for a moment.

"Ah," the Healer said. "You druen are indeed all the same. Goodbye. I shall not mend your wounds, blood-drinker. You have shown me you do not deserve it." He turned and left. Samari, knowing he could never overpower the Healer in his weak state, walked the opposite way, toward "the King's outpost"—no doubt, Dundari.

~

Samari hobbled down the wide, packed-dirt path. Every few miles, a small inn or house opened up along the way, inviting travelers; but they would not accept him. At his slow rate—hobbling, at best, ten miles a day—the journey lasted four days before a telltale column of smoke arose above the trees. By then, snow had piled on the boughs of the pines, and lay an inch thick over the road. Samari was shaking with hunger, barely able to walk, by the time he came to the sight of the great burning.

The walls of the city had been removed, golden brick by golden brick. Seven distinct piles of bodies—perhaps thirty feet high—roasted along with the houses and shops that had been razed to their foundations. Along the perimeter of where the wall once had been, heads had been placed on sticks. The army of King Homar, thousands strong, surrounded the perimeter of the burning city where they had laid their camps, or busied themselves sowing the outlying land with salt. *A scene of total victory*, Samari thought, but in his weakness and hunger could not summon the energy to smile. Where the gate once had been, a giant stone sign, ten feet tall, had been etched with Elvish writing:

THE DRUEN NEVER FORGET.

Down the road, a cadre of Blood Knights rode toward Samari, their crimson capes flapping in the wind.

"Dark One's eyes," Samari rasped to himself, "I will be glad to get some food and water."

"Who goes there?" a Blood Knight demanded, hand resting on his sword-hilt.

"Samari," he answered. "I was with a boat that crashed."

"Ah, yes," the Blood Knight answered. "Many weeks ago… your fellow-soldiers said there was a deserter that left them to die."

"No," Samari wheezed. "No… they… I can explain—"

"Come with me!" the Blood Knight snapped.

~

King Homar stood in the midst of the blackened ash of Dundari, as his soldiers walked around, ensuring no bit of the former town remained standing. Nearby was Gilthari, bow and quiver strapped to his back. His eyes lit up and a wide wolfish grin spread over his face.

Samari dropped to one knee. "Homar son of Homar... friend."

"Samari. My subject."

The word stung. "I am sorry."

"Quiet," answered the king. "You have done a most ignoble thing. And a foolish thing as well. Your friends, your fellow-soldiers, managed to fight off the ill-armed, ill-prepared inbreds who live south of Nardur. But you fled combat, deserted them, even though they were soon-after rescued by a ship."

"I am sorry—"

"Quiet," answered the king. "You are a traitor to both me and your fellow-soldiers. You are a traitor, and you shall receive a traitor's death."

"Friend..."

"Subject," the king intoned. "You look truly awful. Your leg is useless; perhaps if you were healthy you could make a case for me keeping you alive. But you are worthless to me. You are a traitor, and you deserve a traitor's death."

"Friend..." The word tasted false to him as soon as it left his lips.

By dusk the cross was ready for him—three giant wooden boards, two crossing each other to form an "X." He thought of Malirias and how in truth it was him that deserved this, the runaway slave whose faithlessness he had announced before the ship's crew. *This is not the way a freeman soldier should die*, he thought. *But in the end this is how I shall pass from the world.*

The thousands and thousands of soldiers stood there and watched. None were smiling, save Gilthari.

"This is the punishment for desertion!" King Homar roared. "Whenever you are tempted to leave your brothers-in-arms, to abandon your fellow-soldiers for the sake of your own life, remember that this is how yours will end. Know it is better to die in combat than to live as a coward. Forever sear this image in your mind; and it shall guard you against a similar fate. Neither the king, nor his agents, will ever show a deserter mercy."

Men were approaching Samari with hammers and nails. He screamed like he'd never screamed before, even before the first blow landed. He screamed, and neither god nor man nor Dark One answered.

CHAPTER FIVE:
TRIUMPH

From the mouth of the Black River to the gates of Druenel-Hai, a crowd lined either side of the one-mile march. Carts rattled by, piled with silver and gold coins laden with ceremonial braziers of burnished bronze, marble statues and various curios for art-collectors. More carts went on down the prescribed path, piled high with spidersilk robes dyed flame-orange and blood-red, or stuffed with paintings of watercolor and ink printings. Another, packed tight with priceless codices and scrolls of ancient history and science, would surely end its triumphal procession in the ever-expanding Library of Druthor. To the crowd's surprise—when the booty on display ended with an enormous gilded statue of King Danthemari—no newly-won slaves made an appearance, for King Homar had butchered all the residents of Dundari.

After the dozens of carts filled with loot rattled by, a squadron of Blood Knights trotted down the road; a horn blew, and the official procession began as the soldiers made their way toward the capital city of vampire-kind. Riding a giant destrier of midnight-black, King Homar rode high above his lesser men-of-war, bearing *Lifedrinker*, the vampire blade, in his right hand. At the sight of him, the crowd burst into cheers. But among the common folk watching the display, a sense pervaded that this great slaughter was only the beginning; that indeed, one day all the elves under sun and moon would call the vampire king their lord.

DAY OF RECKONING

Druthas, Chief Advisor

As a rule, vampire lords do not die in serene nobility and peace; but King Homar, son of Homar, of the House of Allenon, proved a rare exception. His dying words—"Let my son rule"—he spoke with almost shocking calm.

Druthas—chief advisor to the king and his Blood Court; frequent witness to the murders, tortures and decadence of the Black Castle—at times wondered whether the dying sovereign had found religion in his twilight years. Such a thing would be the ultimate scandal in the Dark Land, where the mere mention of the gods spelled ostracism or worse; and if King Homar, son of Homar—the Prince of Dread who leveled Dundari and enriched Nardur at the expense of the lesser nations—had found solace in idle promises of Heaven, and worshipped the Many Faces of Light, then he had acted with exceptional wisdom not to mention it to anyone in the Blood Court, or even (perhaps especially) his wife.

Masomé, that harridan, exemplified all the bad qualities of the druen race. She spent a quarter of the tax-revenue on fine spidersilk gowns, lace undergarments and golden jewelry. Indeed, she had purchased so many outfits she had one for every day of the year. Homar son of Homar, now a nearly-blind old man of three hundred years, had no awareness of her scheming and her lavish and luxuriant behavior. She lived only for the exaltation of the druen lords and ladies, savoring their amazed gasps at her extravagant attire; and the pleasures of blood, and of the bed. Indeed she had borne King Homar, son of Homar, a rightful heir—the crown prince, Samon—as well as two princesses soon-ready for marriage, but in truth, with the company she kept, who knew if their father was truly King Homar?

Masomé, ever the actress, shed tears as the *drazzandori* gave his final breaths. She wore one of the fine spidersilk gowns—dyed a deep scarlet and inset along the golden hems with sapphires—which she had purchased from the southlanders.

If we sold her wardrobe, Druthas thought to himself, *we could pay all the nation's expenses for a decade.*

Her teary eyes met Druthas' and he wondered if she could read his thoughts, if she could detect his hatred for her. The thought sent gooseflesh tearing across his skin. He had seen what she did to the castle slaves and common servants who looked at her without due deference. One servant-boy who broke a crystal cup, she had lathed in butter and tossed to her menagerie of snow bears.

A woman in the black attire of an antipriest stood at the foot of the royal bed. Her presence and her title was a mere formality; the antipriests no longer laid sacrifices before the Black Altar. Though the druen did not revere the gods, few thought it acceptable to give the Dark One any equivalent reverence.

Masomé walked over to the side of her husband's bed, laid an ivory hand on his wrist. "He is dead." She could produce tears at will, but her speech held no trace of sadness. "My dear husband, Homar, the greatest lord the druen have ever seen. He will be dearly missed."

Not by you, Druthas would guess.

"With the passing of the king, the crown shall pass to his son," Masomé said. "But he is not of age. And in the interim I will rule."

The antipriest's lips pursed into a line; her eyes met Masomé's, shallow with fear even as she quite obviously tried to hide all weakness. "You speak truth, my dear Masomé. The crown shall pass to you."

Masomé's face hardened. "There some things left to be done. There are wrongs that need righting." Her dagger-hard eyes bored into Druthas', seething with fury. "Druthas, chief advisor, my husband loved you better than anyone else in the Blood Court. With your toadying words you gained his favor, yet always in the background you served yourself. I hear you speaking of me in the shadows of the castle; you tried your best to poison me against my husband. You are a serpent, Druthas. Few have remained in the Blood Court's shadow for as long as you have; always thinking of your self-preservation you remained in a place high above your station."

"Your Grace." Druthas fell to his knees, weak. "I have always been your faithful servant. I have never spoken ill of you. I have never thought ill of you." Tears fell, showing weakness—the ultimate sin in the Black Castle, the death-knell which the Blood Court followed like hungry sharks. "I beg of you." Beg, a word never spoken in the Blood Court by any wise man. "Please, Masomé, I have always done my best to serve you. I have always—"

"Silence!" Masomé hissed. "You followed my husband Homar like an adoring puppy, and my husband—as is so typical of him—returned your affection with his trust. But the closer you grew to him, the more distant he grew from me."

The antipriest had gone rigid, not daring to move a single muscle in her body.

"I have witnesses," Masomé said. "Witnesses that show you were attempting to murder me, to conspire against the very Queen of the Vampires. How dare you! How dare you?"

"Lies!" Druthas sobbed.

"You accuse me of lying?" She turned her head. "Come in!"

Through the door, members of the Blood Court—all of whom he recognized, many whom he considered friends—walked in with wolfish expressions on their faces. There was Malorron, the court singer; Benthelon, War Advisor whom he considered a friend; Niamé, the woman he had loved.

"You, too, Niamé?" Druthas wept.

Niamé returned his desperation with a smile. "Me, too. You thought I was disloyal to the queen… you dared ask me to poison her wineglass."

"Lies!"

"You gave me a dagger," Malorron said, "and told me to stick it in the queen's chest while she slept."

"Dark One take you, liar!"

"I heard you speak ill of her, trying to turn her own husband against her," Benthelon intoned.

"You are liars! You are all liars!" Druthas half-sobbed, half-screamed.

"That would not hold up before a judge," Masomé said, "if we even needed one. But we do not—the queen's edict, with the agreement of the antipriest beloved-of-the-Dark-One, is law."

"Yes!" the antipriest stammered. "Yes, the evidence is c-conclusive!"

"Very well," answered Masomé. "As payment for high treason, he will lose his life."

Druthas continued to weep. "Gods damn you... gods damn you."

A hush fell over the room. "He dares to invoke the gods," Masomé said. "He dares to invoke the ones by which the southerners shame us. His ill judgment will not go unpunished."

~

In front of the royal castle, in the shadow of the ebon-black statue of Prince Gilden, the queen's servants heated up a giant bronze kettle while the slaves and subjects in the town square watched. As the kettle itself began to glow, Druthas' tears fell, and sputtered incoherent prayers.

Some showed disapproval as Druthas was burnt to death in the searing-hot metal, while others watched it like they might a street-musician; most watched with the callous indifference for which the druen had become famous, caring nothing for Druthas' life or death, either way.

CHAPTER ONE:
THE TROUBLE BEGINS

From one mouth to another, along the network of roads, news of the outsiders' arrival spread from its starting-point where Black River met the sea. The news grew more fanciful with each telling—first the truth, a small group of blond Lamen officials had arrived, then a large group of soldiers attacked, then an army had invaded. Only in the capital, where the emissaries—sent by King Estilas El-Bendori himself—entered with the typical Lamen bravado, did they know the whole truth.

~

Lamdas Luaddon, dó kentari

At the gates of the Black Castle, a contingent of vampires wearing heavy steel-plated armor and flowing crimson capes, glared at Lamdas and his royal contingent with the expected shock and anger. They had come—it would seem to the blooddrinkers—unarmed, but all Lamdas needed to protect himself was the staff in his hands.

"I wish to request an audience with the lord of Nardur, Homar Allenon," Lamdas said, and he had no doubts his lack of fear unsettled them more than anything.

"If you ever intend to speak with the ruler of Nardur," one of the warriors growled, unsheathing a sword of cold steel, "then you shall address him by his proper title, king."

"There is only one true King of the Elves, my good sir, but I shall call Homar 'king' if he wishes," Lamdas said, and at his words the other dozen warriors drew their swords. "Nonetheless, I am sent on behalf of the true King of the Elves, and on behalf of the Lord of the Lonen, Aimon, who also calls himself 'king.' I wish to speak to King Homar Allenon at once."

"A bold man you are, to come to the land of your mortal

enemy, and request to speak with him when you are so badly outmatched and outnumbered," the warrior growled. "Nonetheless, Homar has gone on to the grave."

The news delighted Lamdas but he made sure not to show it. This would bode well for King Estilas' plans.

"The crown prince is thirteen years old. While he matures, his mother rules in his stead."

"I should like to speak to the lovely woman."

"Would you?" the warrior sneered. "I am not certain the feeling will be returned."

"I would love to find out."

The warrior's eyes narrowed. "My Blood Knights will keep watch over you to see that you don't escape; it is anyone's guess if the queen will send you away in disgrace, or butcher you on the Black Altar."

But Lamdas did not fear; not even the Queen of the Vampires would be such a fool.

Minutes later the warrior returned, and led them into the Black Castle.

~

The Crimson Throne did not disappoint Lamdas in size or in shock. The red cloth had the dark color of blood, and the woman who sat upon it did just as much to strike terror in passersby: a woman of bloodless-white, ivory skin and a kind of sharp and severe beauty, with the black eyes of a soulless killer.

"On the first day of my reign the do-gooders come to wish me well—blond hair, bright clothing, and all. An ominous sign for me, I'd say. Perhaps I should abdicate right now."

"Perhaps you should," Lamdas said, and in an instant became aware of the danger he was in—the vampire queen leapt to her feet, snarling. "The most noble King Estilas, El-Bendori, the Good Lord, has remembered the slaughter you induced upon the innocent town of Dundari. He sees the treasures you stole, the wells you poisoned, and the total ruin you created—but most importantly, he sees the innocent lives you cut short… man, woman, and child. Long, long ago, during the reign of Gilesti Danirias, the Eternal King himself granted you a charter of freedom, but you have grievously broken the terms of the agreement. You have gone beyond the border he outlined; you have repaid our mercy with slaughter."

The queen of the vampires howled with laughter.

"Long, long ago a servant of the Lonen was stricken nearly-dead—a sorceress from the Iron Isle who had come to offer you help—but though immobile and paralyzed for the remainder of her too-short life, she told the 'king' Aimon of your people's great wickedness. Therefore, an unprecedented thing has happened, to put an end to the vampire nation forevermore. His Celestial Majesty, King Estilas El-Bendori, and the Lonen 'King' Aimon the Fifth, declare war upon the vampire nation, and revoke its right to exist. Within a matter of weeks, expect the armies of the Eternal King and the armies of the Lonen at your doorstep."

"Kill them!" the queen of the vampires shrieked, and the Blood Knights flanking her charged.

Nimbly, Lamdas and his fellow dó kentari bounded out of the castle's confines, staves in hand.

~

Masomé, Drazzandoré

The gall of these southlanders! Masomé wrung her hands, beside herself and overcome with nausea. *The gall of my husband, to get me into this horrid mess and then die.* She loathed her husband more than she ever had. She had lived a life of luxury and creature comforts, and to think that she—Masomé, lady of the castle—would command a war, she could not begin to fathom. She wanted to vomit, thinking of how it would all unfold.

She thought of her son, whom she loved more than her own life, and how unused he was to trouble of any kind. She had provided him the best swords-training of anyone in Nardur, but trouble—true trouble—was beyond him. She had given Homar a son in his twilight years, long-after the wars and battles he was known for.

For once in her entire life, Masomé felt utterly vulnerable and alone.

CHAPTER TWO:
BEST-LAID PLANS

Masomé, Drazzandoré

Under the dread specter of war, Masomé ate with the court in the Hall of Feasting. Wine-cups filled with blood were a sign of distress, of a need to soothe tightly-wound nerves. Her son Samon had already gulped down his blood and now picked apart his pan-fried haddock with his hands; none dared to correct him, at the threat of Masomé's wrath. Looking at Malorron, Benthelon, and Niamé, she realized how very much she loathed these people. Anyone so eager to turn on their friends for their own self-preservation—even at Masomé's direction—had no mettle or character, and if the time seemed right they'd turn on her. But she would not punish them for obeying her... at least, not yet.

Dark One's eyes, I wish I had thrown those three in the bronze kettle, and not Druthas. But it was too late to change course. She had thrown Druthas into the kettle, not these three faithless worms. *And now the southern do-gooders and their gods will have us all thrown into a kettle of their own design.*

"What shall we do?" Masomé finally said. They looked up at her attentively, like well-behaved dogs. *All they care about is surviving me— and their behavior is a monster that I have bred.*

"Whatever you do, I am sure it will succeed," Niamé said with a smile that disgusted her.

"I wish you'd have a helpful thought, Niamé... actual advice, rather than self-serving praise. Dark One's eyes, I'd like to thrust that fork into your heart sometimes."

Niamé looked up at her and went stiff. "Of course, Your Grace. I will try to think."

"Perhaps you shouldn't bother." Niamé, once, had cleaned the palace and cooked meals as a common maidservant, but her diligence and polite manners had convinced Masomé to appoint her mistress over all the maidservants. She dared not speak ill of Masomé, just like the rest of him.

This behavior, she reminded herself, *is a monster I have created.*

Across the table, her chubby son smacked his lips and spit out fishbones, sometimes into the faces of his fellow diners.

His poor manners were a monster she had bred, too. For a while they continued to eat in silence, chewing or taking sips of their blood, but Masomé had all but lost her appetite.

"Your Grace, I should mention something," Benthelon said, "which I have neglected to tell you. Do you remember the pretender, Drathanyi, who tried to wrest the Crimson Throne from your husband?"

Masomé felt her gaze harden.

"Drathanyi, the Bandit King, who won many battles against your husband Homar, before the general Dancari killed him?"

"What are you speaking of?"

"Well, I should mention, dearest Masomé, that he has returned out of hiding..."

"Hiding?" Masomé began. "You said——"

"I said many things, Masomé, because I feared you." Benthelon's lips formed an impudent smile. "Drathanyi and his bandit legion have waited north of Nardur in the Ever-Ice, for the past three years. They have crossed the border. Drathanyi the Bandit King is alive and well, with an army of some ten thousand soldiers marching under him, and the support of many of the lesser lords. He will be in the city tonight—I have arranged the gates to stay open."

The food turned in Masomé's stomach, becoming sour and sickening.

"He is not as strong a man as Homar, though he is close," Benthelon went on. "But he is ten-thousand times the man you have trained your son to become—the spoiled, chubby halfwit. And besides, who knows for certain who that monster's father is?"

"How dare you?" Masomé at last shrieked. "Guards!"

"I hear the Bandit King is fair of form, tall and menacing," Niamé purred. "I dream of him sometimes, with a sword buckled to his side. How handsome he will look, with *Lifedrinker* in his possession."

The footsteps of the approaching castle guards echoed through the feasting hall, but they could not stave off Masomé's nausea.

"Tonight, I think I will compose a song," Malorron said, wineglass of blood in hand. "The death of the chubby halfwit and his scheming mother. You have brewed the bitter draught of death for so many in your household, Masomé, so I wonder how it will feel when you taste it."

"No! Guards!"

"I wonder how close the Bandit King is to the capital, now. Surely, he is almost at its doorstep," Niamé kept purring. "I can envision him now. The gates will open; the folk of Druenel-Hai welcoming him as their sovereign... me, welcoming his embrace."

The doors to the Feasting Hall opened, and a dozen Blood Knights flooded in. "Kill them!" Masomé shrieked. "Kill these faithless traitors to the realm."

"Kill the faithless traitors to the realm, you say," the voice of the Blood Knight grandmaster Gimonari said from above her. "We shall do exactly that. Imari, you take care of the precious Crown Prince. I will deal with Masomé."

"Wait," Masomé breathed, "I beg of you."

"A bronze kettle, will it be?" Niamé said. The druen maid, a plump, saucy girl of barely twenty, leaned a bit closer to her queen. "Only the most noble and fitting death for you; to see you drink the draught you poured for so many others."

"No," Benthelon sneered. "That would be too much effort. We must have time to sell her wardrobe... with all the funds we'll rake in we could hire a mercenary force the size of Nardur itself."

"You dare not," Masomé growled, though the strength was long-gone from her voice, and she felt cold. "You could not..."

"We will," Malorron said.

A Blood Knight laid his sword-blade across the crown prince's neck.

"The child is blameless," Masomé wailed. "Please do not hurt him. If you must kill someone, kill me alone." Still she shut her eyes, hearing the slicing of flesh along the sword-blade's edge. Then the cold of the sword-edge touched her own neck. "The child is blameless," she repeated.

"Your child is dead," the Blood Knight thundered from above her. "He is a lost cause, my sweet."

"Do not call me 'your sweet.' I am far above your station."

"Even at the threshold of death," the Blood Knight said, "she is incapable of common kindness. History will not look well on you, my darling sweet."

The cold metal ran across her neck, opening her throat.

CHAPTER THREE:
INTO THE NORTH

Elesté, Chief Healer, Amandoré

Elesté—the Chief Healer of all the Lamen people—had never traveled so far in her life. Nor had she ever expected the true Elven King and the eastern pretender Aimon, lord of the Dark Elves, to ever work with anything approaching cooperation. But at last the ship had docked in the windblown, iced-over hell of a town called Port Andom. It was a mere port of call—the army would make its landing much further north, in a small natural bay where they would begin their march to the land of the foul blooddrinkers—but Elesté had expressly ordered the sailors to allow a night here. A war could not be won without the grace of the gods—the Many Faces of Light—but neither could they win a war without wisdom and foreknowledge. And of all the places outside Nardur, it seemed this ramshackle town of five-thousand persons would hold the most knowledge of the vampire race.

In the town, where fishmongers hawked their nets full of fish and their cages full of crabs, Elesté saw a people dark-featured like the Lonen—as raven-haired as they were white and bloodless—but so too did she notice a subset within the crowd. These people—the vampires—had sharper features than the others and predatory, hunter's eyes. They moved with catlike, sinister grace, and they above all others took notice of Elesté. Some scowled at her; others backed away as if to hide. Her blonde hair and summer-green eyes surely made her stick out in this sea of darkness.

Around her neck, the emerald amulet pulsed with light as it lay across her bare neck, chilling her as it touched her. At all times, she wore the protective ward—forged in the time of Danthelon Lunitar the Wondersmith—which served as her first defense against evil magic. Yet here, alone—a Lamen lady amid a swarm of the lost and the vagabonds, unarmed save for her white ironwood staff and a crystal wand charged with a blinding-spell—she nonetheless felt more vulnerable than she had in a long while. The emerald might protect her from Forbidden magic, and some machinations of darkness, but it did nothing against common swords and daggers. To answer that, she only had her crystal wand, her kindness and her grace.

A man came walking up to her, clutching a halberd in both hands. His black-whiskered face had a sour, scowling look. "A great lady, you are, judging by your robe."

"No greater or lesser than you, my good man," Elesté answered. "In the eyes of the Light, we are all equally loved, responsible for our choices."

"Oh, stuff it," the man answered, and at his callous words she drew back a moment in shock. "You're a magic weaver, too. Before you cause too much trouble, let me tell you something. My name is Noresti, and I am bailiff, second-in-command to the right lord of Port Andom, Amarion. We have a quite sticky position in this war you've started. By law, we are allies to King Aimon the Fifth, the ruler of Londor. But in truth we are even greater allies with the druen, the ones you called vampires. Without them, we have nothing. They are our foremost trading partners."

"Traders," Elesté said, and tried not to play the judge. "Traders of slaves. Traffickers in the bodies and souls of men."

"Why are you here?" Noresti scowled.

"I had hoped to find an ally in the people of Port Andom. I had hopes... but they have been dashed. It is clear you are dear friends with the King's enemy, the abomination beyond the sea."

"A do-gooder to the last," Noresti answered her. "When you make war on Nardur, sanctimoniously leveling their towns and burning their fields.... Remember, my sweet, of the damage you will wreak on the Free Men of Port Andom. Think of us starving, unable to provide for ourselves in the winter's cold, all because of your self-righteous quest. You think in merely black and white, when there are so many colors. Colors, and shades of gray..."

"If the abomination beyond the sea is destroyed, the southerners will welcome you."

Noresti laughed at her words.

"Surely King Aimon will be glad to have more workers in the

fields…"

"You do not understand anything, do you, high-and-mighty princess? The people of Port Andom are the refuse of the Elven World. Leaving the safety of our town is a death-sentence, most inadvisable. Only here can they escape their fate."

"Refuse, you call yourselves," Elesté said. "Is that a proper name for creations of the Light, even its Firstborn?"

"As I said, stuff it. Your religion will do you no good here, spoiled princess. Though you have done us more kindness than I would have expected…"

"May I speak to your lord?"

Noresti's eyes brimmed with suspicion and distrust. He was a child of the Light like all creation, but he had strayed far from it, into the realm of evil and shadow. As he led her, Elesté said a prayer for him and all the folk of Port Andom—as elves, the Firstborn of creation, yet lost in shadow.

Like the other buildings of the port, the lord's house was built of pinewood. Though sanded, layered in beeswax, and painted light colors inside, it would never have the same architectural magnificence of Danarion and its towers, which seemed sculpted seamlessly by a god's hand.

The Lord of Port Andom was hunched over on his throne chair, clearly indicating some foul injury. His whitish eyes betrayed his near-blindness.

The man is sick, and needs help. Yet the powers of Healing were reserved for the three good elven tribes—the Umen of the forest, the Nurnen of the high hills, and the Lamen of the plain. Only on one rare occasion did Elesté, while serving as Amandoré, use her powers to Heal someone outside that group. A human boy, she remembered, a paralytic whose mother had transported him endless miles to the gates of Danarion; and Elesté had Healed him in direct violation of the King's orders.

"A beautiful wench, it is," the Lord of Port Andom. "Though these old eyes can barely tell a wench from a lad, so I am not altogether certain of her beauty."

"She is neither beautiful nor especially ugly," Noresti asserted, standing by the lord's side.

Elesté suppressed a laugh.

"So tell me, Lamen witch, what it is you want from me."

"The true King of the Elves has amassed an army outside the land of the vampires, what we call the abomination beyond the sea. He intends to remove the Cursed Ones forever, to destroy them totally and ensure they never exist again as a people."

"Grab her," the lord snarled.

Elesté whipped around, seeing two armed guards in Andomasi crabshell helmets stalking toward her, halberds in hand.

"Cut her pretty white throat," the Lord of Port Andom said. "I'd like to see her bleed."

"Wait," Elesté said, feeling the blood drain from her face. She batted the first spearing of the halberd with her Healer's staff; the other she dodged, and it whistled through the air uncomfortably close to her face.

"Why should I wait, my sweet?" the Lord of Port Andom said.

"Because…" she launched herself backward, to the edge of the throne. She grabbed hold of the lord's face, and he tried to bite her. A flash of white-gold light danced at the edge of her fingertips; the air chilled, she drew back her hand, and the Lord of Port Andom's eyes lost all their dull whiteness. He righted himself in his chair, no longer in his crippled position.

But his soldiers kept running toward her; one hacked with the halberd, and she brought her Healer's staff to meet it. He had struck so hard she fell to the floor, easy prey for the next blow.

"Stop!" the Lord of Port Andom said, and stood to his feet nimbly, like a man of twenty. "This wench has done me a great service. And she is a quite fetching woman, Noresti. Never lie to me again."

"I won't."

Elesté stood to her feet and caught her breath. She met the lord's gaze with her best show of strength. Still she was vulnerable, at the mercy of these Andomasi criminals save for the crystal wand, still hooked in her belt. "Your Lordship." She bowed her head.

"I will hear you out," he answered, and again assumed his seat in the throne chair. "I have not seen this well since... *I have never seen this well.* I feel I am in a different world... the Otherworld, with its brilliant colors."

Elesté circumvented the throne chair to stand in front of him. "The Otherworld is a wonderful place, it is said; but its gates and portals are nearly all closed, and not even the Fair Folk have escaped the Dark One's corrupting taint."

"Speak," the Lord of Port Andom demanded.

And she did. "The vampires were cursed for the great evil of their forefather, and his legacy of cruelty and wickedness lives on in his children. Many years ago the vampires leveled the innocent town of Dundari, slaughtered all its residents like sheep.... They did not leave a single of its famous golden bricks standing. They are monsters, Your Lordship, and like monsters they must be hunted to the last, deprived of the very lives they steal. It would be a mercy to the world, to see them eradicated."

"Would it be a mercy to them?"

"They do not show mercy to anyone else."

"And this from a Lamen princess!"

"I am not the daughter of the King, or even an elf-lord..."

"Know that when you take all these lives, Lamen princess—when you spurn the commands of mercy and the teachings of Solarion to eradicate an entire people, when you watch the soldiers cut the necks of vampire-babes and send the vampire-women fleeing from the burning towns—"

The words themselves merely stung her, but the images the words conjured struck her like a blow.

"Know, when you sit in the midst of a land red with blood—even the blood of your enemies, the one you call an abomination beyond the sea—think of us, the common criminals of Port Andom, and know that when you slay the helpless people of Nardur, that you are destroying us as well. The Lamen despise slavery—they despise us, thinking themselves always as the pinnacles of virtue. But your lovingkindness and goodness is poison to those you deem unworthy."

"Your words disarm me," Elesté said. "I fear the King has made up his mind; and I shall have no recourse but to act according to his will. Estilas El-Bendori is a wise and vigorous man but he is strong-headed. He will not rest until the vampire race is extinguished, and I fear I cannot change him."

"Then you are my enemy," the Lord of Port Andom said. "You have healed my afflictions... I can see like an eagle... but my quality of life is nothing compared to the survival of my people. Begone, Lamen witch."

"I... I am sorry... I cannot—" Elesté stammered.

"Go!" the Lord of Port Andom boomed like thunder. "Destroy us all, and remember our starving, frozen faces as you work your witchcraft."

"I—"

"Go!"

As if by magic, the word sent Elesté scrambling backward. She left the lord's home breathless, wondering how such vagabonds had changed her. The Druen Curse—the thirst for blood—was punishment enough, sent by the Light itself. The Light had not commanded them to exterminate the druen; King Estilas had, compelled by the ravaging of Dundari.

The petty lord's words had changed her; but she could not, and would not, disobey her liege.

CHAPTER FOUR:
THE BANDIT KING

Niamé, Mistress of the Maidservants

The tales of Drathanyi did not disappoint Niamé in the slightest when the so-called Bandit King at last arrived. He was at least six feet tall, towering above the people of the court, with shoulders so broad he could scarcely move through the doors. A thick white scar ran across his face—a trophy from his battles with King Homar—and his hard face did not change at all, reflecting no emotion even in view of the opulence of the royal castle.

Thick leggings of boiled leather went down to his muscular white calves, and iron-lined boots clanked on the tile floor as he walked. A cuirass of boiled leather covered his chest, crafted in the shape of muscles Niamé did not doubt Drathanyi had. Most impressive of all to Niamé, the sheath of a greatsword hung from his belt all the way down to the floor. Only a man of vast powers of strength could wield such a weapon in combat. As he entered the throne room, Niamé fell to her knees.

"All hail King Drathanyi!" she called out to him, but he did not so much as turn back. Instead, as all the courtiers and Blood Knights within the room followed Niamé's move, he instead wordlessly walked up to the Crimson Throne itself, and took his rightful place.

If only he had come at a better time, Niamé reflected. Niamé merely oversaw the maidservants, but rumors had reached them. The southern do-gooders had been spotted across the sea; the small druen navy had not even attempted to sink the bulky southern warships. The specter of war hung heavy over them. Some subjects of the Narduren Crown claimed that they deserved it; that they had turned their backs on the gods, and why then should they expect to live? In a more peaceful time, such words would spell immediate execution; but the druen needed every spare hand, or the do-gooders would complete their mission.

~

Malorron

A month had passed since Drathanyi had taken the throne. By any wise person's judgment, he had done all the right things. Everything of iron he had melted down to craft weapons; he had armed even the lowest of his subjects. He had summoned the leader of the Black Zealots and convinced the order that the cause was worth fighting for. He had melted all the luxurious items of gold to pay for war expenses; he had sent a half-dozen subjects to sell the wardrobe of the dead queen Masomé.

But in the eyes of Niamé, the saucy man-eater, he had done everything wrong. Drathanyi had spurned her advances for the sake of his absent wife, sending her into a near-hysterical rage. To Malorron, it was delightful to see. As for him, he did his duties as chief singer and musician, but Drathanyi was not a man of the arts, and he did not listen for long. Almost all of his time he spent on planning for the war. Spies had come with regular frequency to the court—an army of at least forty-thousand soldiers, three-quarters Lamen and one-quarter Lonen—massed about five miles south of Sardur, the country of the inbred Hill Cannibals.

The Elven King, Estilas, had come personally with a full array of healers, lightbearers, Stag Riders of Non, auxiliary archers of Umdar, and the best veterans of Lamdar. The Lonen ruler, Aimon the Fifth, had sent his son the Crown Prince in his stead, several thousand halberdiers, and a contingent of nearly one-hundred magic weavers: sorcerers, the spies said, from the Blood Keep; and sorceresses from the Iron Isle.

At best, all the trained troops of Nardur amounted to half the enemy's number; the Blood Knights numbered a bit more than a thousand, and the trained vampire soldiers several times that.

"Our only hope," Malorron heard Drathanyi say on a number of occasions, "is to outwit them."

It was a day in late spring, while a light snow had begun to fall, when the news reached them that the armies of the Elven King had set out. And with that, Drathanyi and his armies—massed in and around Druenel-Hai—left southward to meet them.

~

Benthelon, War Advisor

Benthelon left with King Drathanyi, quite clearly at his wit's end. The lord of the druen would not listen to him; Benthelon knew full-well that fighting the do-gooders would be a disaster. The only way out was to prostrate themselves before the Elven King and beg for his mercy, pay an annual tribute no matter how exorbitant. "It is a small price to pay," Benthelon had said, "and gods know I won't lose my life trying to fight them."

"Ha!" Drathanyi had laughed the prior night, "Yes! Yes, you will! I shall ensure it."

And against protocol, the Bandit King had forced Benthelon along with the army, to die or live along with them.

"Try to escape," the Bandit King had said, "and I will disembowel you."

Benthelon wished more than ever for Masomé. For all her flaws at least she cared enough about her life not to commit tactical suicide. Though Benthelon had been a major orchestrator in her demise, and had picked the Bandit King as a competent successor, he now realized what a truly wretched mistake he had made.

There is nothing worth dying for, Benthelon had told himself. *I could be wrong.* Early on in his life he had determined he would do whatever it took to keep it, but—Dark One's eyes!—this Bandit King did not value intelligence, wisdom, and self-preservation. Instead, he valued valor and sacrifice and all the unintelligent values that the do-gooders revered. And now, Benthelon—who had preserved his life through all of Masomé and Homar's terrors, who had betrayed his first wife and his friend, and in return lived to the ripe age of ninety-five—had earned the enmity of this barbarian in his midst. A monster he had created, but one that had nothing but hatred for him. Throughout the whole of the long march, the giant hulk Drathanyi spared no opportunity to roughhouse him, nearly knocking him over.

There is nothing worth dying for; I could be wrong. Throughout the day's journey he looked often for a way of escape, but nothing ever presented itself. In all it seemed he was doomed to get on Drathanyi's good side, to feign the part of a brave warrior, or otherwise ensure Drathanyi placed him far behind the soldiers, so that when the slaughter ensued he had a chance to run and hide. Perhaps, he thought with a smile, he could see a stag rider's lance pierce Drathanyi straight through, breaking through flesh and bone. He'd rejoice at the sight.

Dusk fell late, as it did in spring, and they had come near the southern border. In the distance, Benthelon at last made out the enemy's front lines: the legendary mounted combatants of Non, riding on giant stags that could bowl over horses with their antlers. At the sight, his stomach turned, and his old heart picked up pace. He was not ready to die; no intelligent person was ever ready to die. Only the stupid sacrificed themselves for a cause. He turned a slight bit and tried to back away. A giant fist—Drathanyi's—slammed him from behind, stole all the air from his lungs, and sent him sprawling onto all fours. The blow had drained all the air from him; so much so he truly couldn't speak or manage to insult the hulking imbecile that lurked above him.

"A coward is the lowest of all criminals," Drathanyi's dull, stupid voice boomed. "But worst of all, he is useless."

"You are useless," Benthelon wheezed, and immediately cursed himself for saying it—he needed to guard his tongue. Weakly he stood up, though it would take him a long while to recover from that ham-fisted strike.

"The strongest soldiers stand in front," Drathanyi blabbered. "The strongest, and the most useless."

No.

"You will learn to be brave, you pathetic worm."

No. No.

"You likely will never learn as much, of course. But the Bandit

King does not reward cowards like you. A man who avoids strife and battle shall be the first to die."

"No!" Benthelon half-screamed, half-gargled. He turned and ran at full-speed, but had barely made one step before the stupid brute's fist hit him again, harder than the first time, breaking his nose and blinding him for several seconds.

~

When the battle began, seconds later, and the Stag Riders of Non began their devastating charge, Benthelon indeed was the first to die. The antlers of a stag bowled him over, sending him flying into the path of another that trampled him underfoot. Choking on blood, crushed and slowly giving in to the forces of death, the guiding words of his life ran again and again through his mind: *There is nothing worth dying for; I could be wrong.*

CHAPTER FIVE:
THE BATTLE OF THE BORDER

Drathanyi, Drazzandori

The Stag Riders of Non proved as fearsome as he had heard. Against beasts so large, with antlers so strong and supple, neither horse nor man could stand in their way; and Drathanyi had instructed his men to draw back and avoid them until they stopped their bucking. Not long after the stag riders' charge ended with the slaughter of many dozen druen and the faltering of Drathanyi's lines, the Black Zealots came tearing in, having shifted into the form of skinless dogs. Only by their power did the first of the great stags lose its life.

Drathanyi bit his lip at the sight of the great stag, its throat torn by the flesh hound's razor teeth, collapsing to the snow packed ground. Its rider managed to leap off his beast and—after a cry of anguished grief—draw two curved daggers, attempting to avenge him in a wild rage. But the Nurnen Elf, warrior though he was, proved the next victim of the wild braying dog.

That was, until a Healer came riding in on a white palfrey—a Lamen woman with an emerald amulet, a white gown, and a magic staff—and thrust her hand forward. Gold magic glittered in her hands, sparkling in an almost whitish-hue; the wounds of the stag sealed, and the beast bucked to life. Another flash of gold magic sparked from her fingertips, and the gutted Nurnen Elf stirred to health, gripping his discarded lance and hoisting himself onto the stag's saddle.

Drathanyi had found his target. He charged the Healer as a second wave of Lamen warriors converged upon them.

Drathanyi had barely made a dozen steps toward the healer before another stag rider met him head-on. The lance would have split his skull but he dodged out of the way artfully, heaving his greatsword back even as the giant stag tossed its head backward, preparing to bowl him over. Instead Drathanyi brought the greatsword down hard, biting several inches into the stag's chainmail-lined head. The beast brayed and huffed, overcome with pain, but still it swept its antlers at Drathanyi. Drathanyi braced himself against the blow and held firm; the blow knocked him off his balance and he stumbled, regaining enough footing to slam the greatsword down harder than ever. This slash bit a few inches deeper, drawing blood; red trickled down its giant muzzle. Drathanyi despised what he had to do, killing such beautiful beast—it was the rider who earned his enmity, but he had no choice.

Drathanyi screamed as he heaved the greatsword, imbuing it with all the strength remaining in his body; the cracking of the antler's skull filled Drathanyi's ears. And then, sure enough, the healer came riding in, fingers glittering with gold-white light, and all the work he had done in an instant reversed itself.

The stag bucked up into its hind legs, its black beady eyes flaring with insatiable rage. Drathanyi ducked past him, and all the anger and hatred in his heart focused in an instant on the healer who had undone all his work.

He ran screaming at her, and at the sight of him her emerald pendant pulsed with green light. From the folds of her yellow spidersilk robe she drew a white crystal wand, obviously simmering with energy. Drathanyi ducked away, forcing his anger to retreat—though maddened with rage a deadly spell no doubt hovered on the tip of that wand.

He cursed the gods he did not believe in. He cursed the Dark One he did not believe in, on whose behalf all this calamity had fallen. Then, beyond the range of the healer, Drathanyi found new prey.

Lonen soldiers, girt in chainmail and wielding halberds, pressed close behind the stag riders, waiting for one of them to fall. The crabshell helmets made no doubts as to their allegiance—Aimon, King of Londor, who had put aside all his hatred for the Lamen Elves to fight the universally despised druen.

He rushed into the front lines, cracking open a crabshell helmet and splitting a soldier's head. He whipped around to land another heavy blow through the chest of another. The Lonen began to scream.

But as he fought, he could not help but notice the druen lines were falling back. He slashed open three more Lonen soldiers, and reluctantly returned to where his own troops fought.

"Onward!" he screamed, lifting his greatsword as it dripped with blood. He wondered if he had erred, if the soldiers would have been more heartened had he fought with *Lifedrinker*, the ancient vampire blade. But he did not have time for hindsight. There was only time to win this battle.

Out of the ranks of the enemy a shrill screech echoed. A titan emerged in their midst: a winged beast with a long neck and a thick spiked tail, reptilian in every way except its smooth, cadaver-white flesh.

Riding on its back, a tenth its size, was the Crown Prince of Londor. Drathanyi had never been much of a reading man, but he had heard rumors—the flying beasts which the kings of Londor bred, which they and they alone could use. The winged beasts of Londor— the White Drakes, they were called—would not even let the king's wife ride on their backs, much less one of his subjects. Only the Lonen royal house in the male line could properly fly them.

The beast rose to a great height, and the druen responded with shock and wonder, and even some of the enemy stopped their fighting to watch. Then the beast descended in a swift glide. Within seconds of its dive it hovered above the heads of the druen warriors; it opened its fanged mouth and green fumes spewed out, filling the air all around with a fetid stench and sickening even Drathanyi.

Arrows flew from druen bows, but they bounced off the hide uselessly. *Not even our swords*, Drathanyi thought to himself, *can slay a drake*. No metal was strong enough... no metal except *estirion*. *Lifedrinker*, the vampire blade forged of starmetal, was stowed in the royal tent. Drathanyi had mastered the greatsword throughout his career as a bandit and ne'er-do-well, not the short blades that weaklings used.

But in truth, he did not have much choice.

"Drathanyi!" shouted the voice of his friend and leading soldier Drasanthi, an archer and incalculable asset to him long ago. "Shall I sound the retreat?"

"Absolutely not," Drathanyi snapped back. "Have I ever in all my life retreated? No, Drasanthi... bring me *Lifedrinker*."

As the druen lines faltered and fell back, Drathanyi remained at the front, attacking the stag riders in a losing battle against the irksome healers. As soon he dealt a rider a devastating wound, it sealed; in all, it seemed they were invincible unless somehow they could slay all the magic weavers of the Lamen King.

The familiar musk of Drasanthi washed over him. He turned and for the first time he could remember, let the greatsword fall from his hands. In its place, he took *Lifedrinker*, its hilt forged in the shape of a skull, its blade a dark blackish color—impossibly hard, yet light as tin. It would take some getting used to.

In the distance, the Lonen king's beast had landed in the midst of the soldiers, and its cadaver-white mouth dripped with blood as it tore druen apart.

"Do not falter, Drasanthi," he told his friend, and bolted toward his foe, the Crown Prince of Londor, and the pet which gave him all his power.

~

The druen had formed a large space around the flying beast, packed tight and unable to flee. The White Drake snapped at them one by one, tearing off heads or crunching steel armor in its teeth.

"Cowards!" Drathanyi roared.

None of the druen stood a chance against it; the archers and crossbowmen shot with decreasing frequency. Their projectiles bounced uselessly off its hide; instead they stood, packed tight from the army, waiting for their turn to die like sheep to the slaughter.

"Cowards!" Drathanyi shouted again, nonetheless, and hid *Lifedrinker*, his *estirion* blade, behind his back. He stepped out into the open, where none dared tread. The White Drake's green reptilian eyes met his. The great beast hissed, yet in those cold orbs Drathanyi saw something like respect.

Riding the White Drake, mounted on a saddle, the Crown Prince of Londor held a short spear and nothing else. His black robes drooped halfway down the White Drake's giant body. His helm of steel wrapped around his head and bared his face to the world—a man of light complexion, compared to the do-gooder Lamen, though not the corpselike hue of the druen; black eyes with an intense stare, examining his challenger.

The White Drake moved to attack and pick off Drathanyi's head, but the Crown Prince of Londor yanked the reigns of his steed, restraining it. "The King of Nardur comes to face me... all while his common-folk soldiers stand back in terror. If only all the folk of Nardur had the king's mettle."

"If only, indeed," Drathanyi answered. "If only all the druen had my courage, the King of Lamdar would be our slave."

"And what would Aimon son of Aimon, Crown Prince of Londor, be?"

"Our friend," Drathanyi answered. "Once I thought the Elven King and the Lonen were mortal enemies... how many wars have there been, between the do-gooders and the so-called Dark Elves?"

"Two great wars, and countless minor ones," the Crown Prince answered, and the White Drake lurched awkwardly as he restrained it. "Yet in truth it is the vampires who are the true Dark Elves. We reject the gods and all other imaginary flights of fancy; you hunger for the blood of sentients. If the Dark One were more than myth, then surely you would be his servant."

"We could be allies, you know," Drathanyi went on. "We could destroy the Lamen together."

"We could," the Crown Prince answered, "but I am not altogether certain it is probable. The Lamen Elves have many Wonders from the prior age... the Lamen armies remain strong, while you falter. I must build my popularity, you see, among the nobles of Londor; and a victory against the backward druen would be as suitable as it is easy."

"Easy, you say," Drathanyi grunted, and kept drawing closer. The invasion no doubt seemed easy to the Crown Prince. If he lost this war, he promised himself he would at least make it difficult.

"What are you hiding behind your back, druen-king?" the Crown Prince said. "Do not think me a fool."

"Come closer, and perhaps you'll find out."

"Come closer, you say," the Crown Prince scoffed, and his beast lurched forward, just barely restrained by the reins. "I tire of you already, druen-king. You have as good as offered yourself as a sacrifice to our patron, the goddess Nothing, and her liege the king, my father. I had hoped you would keep yourself alive a little longer… interest me with your conversation, perhaps even convince me to bring you back, captive, to Naremon. But the high nobles of Londor grow bored with… well, boring, dim-witted people."

"Your Majesty, get back!" a frantic soldier screamed.

Drathanyi inched back—a complete feint, of course, but the Crown Prince bought it. The White Drake snapped its jaws at Drathanyi in a moment's span, and he answered instantly with a slash of *Lifedrinker*. The *estirion* blade cut through its cadaver-white neck like a normal sword might cut through a man's. Hot blood sprayed him; the drake's giant head hit the hard-packed snow, and the immense body jittered in its death-throes.

The Crown Prince had no time to scream before the excited druen converged upon him with swords and spears. Moments later, a spear had run straight through his chest and a sword had cleaved open a wide crack in his iron helm, splitting his skull. The Crown Prince of Londor had gone on to his patron, Nothing; Drathanyi hoped she would be good to him.

He eyed *Lifedrinker*. He had underestimated the sword; despite his lack of practice, it had won the day against the Crown Prince.

But not against the others, he reflected, as the druen lines continued to fall back.

Drunk on dragon-blood the men around Drathanyi fought harder and more energetically than their compatriots. Yet the Stag Riders of Non continued to press them, backed at all times by the healers; and even as the day grew late and the sun darkened, the luminous spells of the lightbearers kept the battlefield as bright as day. Beyond the few they had slain, thousands more awaited.

Drathanyi gave the signal to retreat. There was no glory in running, but if he did not retreat and regroup within the walls of the Black Castle, then his cause would fail. It was better to be a dishonorable victor than an honorable failure.

As they turned and rode off, or ran in a hundred different

directions, the shouts of a Lamen general echoed all around them. "The abomination beyond the sea will soon be extinguished! The godless will perish as they well deserve! Onward!"

Perhaps they were godless—monsters, even—but against those whom they deemed godless, the god-fearers inflicted just as much cruelty as their enemies displayed. Drathanyi dealt a stag one blow, healed instantly; then another, healed again; and at last clove off its head. The stag fell, and the stag rider with him. For once, the healer's magic failed them.

The healer on the white horse, wearing an emerald amulet, stood behind him. Her summer-green eyes reflected a woman sad and regretful.

From the site of the battle, the army made at first an ordered, and then a frenzied retreat. In all, it seemed the war was lost. Drathanyi mounted the horse of a fallen Blood Knight, and with *Lifedrinker*—still dripping red with drake's-blood—in hand, he rode hard into the deepening night.

When he reached the streets of Druenel-Hai, the normally reasoned if dispassionate locale he knew had turned into a scene of frenzy. Some dealt with the news by locking their doors; others fled, hoping to hide or perhaps leave Nardur altogether. But Drathanyi knew the Lamen King had an All-Seeing Orb in his possession and—though using them came with great spiritual risk—he could, if necessary, peer through every thicket and locked home in Varda. So too did he have other Wonders of the prior age, which would spell their certain doom.

I am the druen king, he thought. *I must lead.* It was a far cry from what he had been just years ago—a rebellious bandit hated throughout Nardur, except for the vampire lords who saw beyond the rumors to his talent.

Soldiers—Blood Knights on armored warhorses, common footmen lucky enough to own a steed or lucky enough to steal one—poured through the city gates in waves. The ones without horse had doubtlessly passed on to the grave.

And the Lamen were coming.

Sometime after the sun had fully set and the darkness became complete, King Drathanyi ordered the gatekeepers to shut off entry. In total, perhaps five-thousand soldiers had made it inside. The rest would no doubt die at the hands of the Lamen, unless they took shelter elsewhere.

Out of the Black Castle, the shape of Niamé appeared, her black eyes still seething with resentment. The luscious Mistress of the Maidservants had never been refused before, it appeared. But Drathanyi's wife Admé—hidden in a tower and guarded from the horrors of war—was the only one he wanted. There were few things Drathanyi agreed with the do-gooders about, but one command he did: a man's marital vows should be kept pure.

"Footsoldiers, to the battlements!" Drathanyi roared. "Blood Knights, ready yourselves. Prepare to charge when they break open the gate."

When. He had not intended to reveal the certitude of their failure. But alas, there was little hope for them. He thought of Admé as he scaled the wooden stairs up to the battlements. He was ready to die as a brave warrior and as a king; but he was not ready for Admé to live her life alone.

Then again, the do-gooders intended to kill every last druen. For her sake, Drathanyi stood at the edge of the wall, and waited.

The magic of the lightbearers formed a dawn-like illumination in the horizon. The stag riders no doubt led the charge. Who knew what slaughter they had already wrought, what despair they had already inflicted on the druen—the ones they viewed as inhuman monsters, worthy only of slaying? Soon fire would consume the whole of Nardur.

CHAPTER SIX:
DAY OF RECKONING

The army of the Lamen marched to the foot of Druenel-Hai's walls, as numerous as specks of sand on a beach. The thousands and thousands soldiers could easily encircle the city, each of them well-armed and armored and arrayed in Lamen whites and golds. Drathanyi, standing above the gate, couldn't make out anyone in the thick armor and crabshell helmets of the Lonen, nor were there any red-garbed blood sorcerers or gray-robed iron sorceresses in view. He had slain the Crown Prince of the Lonen; his army had faltered and fallen back. But the Lonen were the least of his two foes—the Lamen now faced the druen, a pack of wolves against a lone deer.

The stag riders had allowed a wide space, an open line through the army. Trumpets blared, and the procession of the Lamen King began.

The so-called True King sallied forth on one of the royal elvish horses, bred in ancient days—a creature white of hair, the size of the largest charger Drathanyi had ever seen yet moving with the grace of the most well-bred showhorse. From its head—armored, as it was, in *estirion* plates—a natural horn protruded, a sharp and supple thing that Drathanyi knew could pierce the thickest of iron plates. The beasts were relics of the prior age, which now seemed an impossibly distant memory; soon all their kind would pass away.

The King's spidersilk robes had a birdlike array of color: deep purples, flame oranges, blood reds, and brilliant yellows, together forming a collective whole—an abstract yet stunning tapestry. The True King, Estilas, had the noble bearing and commanding presence of the prior age. Drathanyi almost drew back at the sight of his stern, commanding blue eyes—eyes that reflected an aloofness and disconnect from the troubles of the mortal world, yet searing in judgment. In his hand, drawn from its sheath, was the King's *estirion* blade—white, unlike *Lifedrinker*'s black, longer and wider.

Drathanyi wondered how many the King's blade had felled. He

wondered how many foes the King himself had slain—probably not many, judging by how little he left the confines of the City of Light.

At his presence the great stags bucked and brayed, trying to hide from his overwhelming presence. His fellow-soldiers dared not even look his way; they treated him as a living god, it seemed, though they would never admit it. Such a thing would be idolatry to the do-gooders—an abomination that only humankind would think of, or perhaps the druen.

Yes, Drathanyi thought. *This man hates the druen.*

His imperious blue eyes met Drathanyi's, and he went cold. "*Drazzandori,* they call you. Lord of the Night. I should not even deign to speak with you, scum. It is more than you allowed the people of Dundari, before you slaughtered them like pigs. Now is come the day of reckoning; you will answer for your crimes, and the abomination-beyond-the-sea will be no more."

Drathanyi wondered what to say. In truth he could say little.

"Surrender unconditionally, and submit to painless deaths," the King hollered. "Or choose wrongly, and we will force it upon you. Either way, you shall get what you so rightly deserve."

"You do-gooders speak so often of mercy and the Light's forgiveness!" Drathanyi answered. "Yet if there is someone whom you think opposes the Light, you slaughter them as eagerly as we ever did!"

The King's imperious blue eyes lost a bit of their fire. His pallid lips twisted—the first change yet in his expression.

"So go ahead, do-gooder!" Drathanyi roared. "Besiege us. Cut down our women and children! I will fight you to the bloody end! And when the gravity of your crime wafts up to Heaven—" The heaven he did not believe in. "—then may your gods cast a pox on your head. A pox on your head, King Estilas! A dread disease on your wife and children, and all your people."

The blue eyes regained all their anger, but the righteous fire did not return.

"Come into our gates! Break down our doors! The druen race will do what you have never done—keep our convictions and promises! We are vile, perhaps, as you say. We are evil. But at least we are not hypocrites."

From the folds of his brilliant robe he drew a white crystal wand, glowing with energy. "The last remaining wand of the prior age, charged with all the primal power of the elemental sorcerers. Know it is by the judgment of the gods that your race is forever extinguished."

That the King possessed a glimmer of magic and ability to tap the power of the wand should not have surprised Drathanyi, but it did. He could only imagine what was to come; the prior age, the Time of the Elves, was a period of heightened magic power.

He reflected on it only a second before the magic burst from the tip of the power of the wand. It blazed like a comet—first red, then gold, then blue—and the crystal shattered to bits. A burst of fire turned the gates to a blazing inferno; a burst of elemental cold streaked out in every direction, spearing by Drathanyi's ears; and then a deafening blast of primal elemental force sent the burning wood and the walls of stone in a hundred pieces, in a hundred directions.

The Blood Knights charged with lances, but Drathanyi knew by all accounts the cause he had fought for was lost. The do-gooders called them self-serving cowards, utterly bereft of all integrity, spineless sea-jellies. Perhaps that was true, for some of them. But if they said all the druen were, then—by the gods he did not believe in—he would prove them wrong.

By the time he reached the ground floor of Druenel-Hai, the Blood Knights had already faltered and several had fallen from their horses, bowled over or pierced by the stag riders.

The King proved himself gallant, charging into the druen ranks alongside his soldiers. Any blows the druen struck were Healed in an instant by the Lamen magic-weavers. It was only moments before all the lines of the druen soldiers broke like leaves in the wind. Then the slaughter began.

The druen-women outside—the homeless or the merely unfortunate—ran as fast as they could away from the ravaging horde. But one by one the stag riders and the Lamen warriors struck them down, civilians and soldiers alike.

The faces of vampire-children poked through windows,

terrified at what was to come. The Lamen showed no mercy. The King lusted for blood. Drathanyi charged a stag rider at the thought of the innocent children of Druenel-Hai. His eyes welled with tears—something that had never happened before. He realized, if this was how the god-fearers acted, he was glad to have never believed in the gods. He cursed the god-fearers and the Light itself. The stag rider began to overpower him; his steed brayed and grunted, preparing to charge and bowl him over or dash Drathanyi's head with its hooves.

A little girl ran screaming from an alley, and a blond Lamen warrior gave chase, a longknife in hand.

How could they claim to be good when they cut a child's throat?

The stag before Drathanyi was braying and huffing, maddened with anger. His rider's face was impossible to see, hidden as it was by a thick helm of steel.

The galloping of hooves echoed throughout the city square. The healer with the blazing emerald pendant had ridden out into the open. Twin tears ran down her cheeks. Her staff fell from her hands. In a voice that echoed across the square, and reverberated through his mind, she screamed: "Is this what the Light commands you to do, O King Estilas? To slaughter children and babes? If this is what the Light commands, I will serve Shadow. In any case you were wrong about something."

The King looked back at her incredulously, pausing from his attack and letting his prey—a young woman—escape.

"There is one wand remaining from the prior age, of such power the brittle crystal could scarcely contain it."

What she shouted next reverberated clearly in Drathanyi's mind, but it was a shout of thought and not of voice: *Druen, vampires, children of the night, shield your eyes!*

A wand was in her hand, and Drathanyi obeyed her command, shielding his vision. Even covered with his arm and his thick leather sleeves, the blaze of light was visible to him.

When the flash faded, and he removed his arm from his eyes, the Lamen army—all of them—stumbled around like blind men.

"Elesté! Traitor!" King Estilas screamed.

"Elesté!" Drathanyi responded. "Savior."

The vampire army, now only a thousand strong, converged upon the helpless host. Estilas succumbed to the first blow. His robe would fetch a wondrous price among the traders of Port Andom. The stag riders, also blinded, charged aimlessly. One crashed headlong into a stone building and fell from his steed.

The tides turned in an instant. The common soldier who stabbed King Estilas dropped his bloody sword. "Today I shall feast on King's blood!" he shouted, and sank his fangs into the Elven King's fair neck.

The druen soldiers charged the blinded prey, and now it was the Lamen that fell liked lambs to the slaughter. Even the healers, now, were blind, and the druen rushed to drink deeply from their veins—a rumor persisted that a magic-weaver's blood tasted best of all.

"Stop!" Drathanyi ordered faintly, but the madness of bloodthirst had consumed them.

Elesté, the woman who had betrayed her people, to whom the vampires owed their now-certain victory, screamed and ran up the scaffolding toward the battlements. Drathanyi followed her the whole way.

She wailed in anguish. When she reached the stone of the battlements, she dropped her healer's staff. "Light forgive me!" she screamed. "I am a traitor and I shall receive a traitor's death! My compassion is cruel!"

"Elesté!" Drathanyi cried as he too set foot on the battlements. "You have not done anything wrong."

"O Light, if you consign me to eternal punishment—then know I did not intend to err. Light forgive me!" She moved to leap off the wall to her death, but Drathanyi grabbed her. "Lay off me, blood drinker." Her green eyes were watering, yet wide and burning with condemnation.

"Think of all the innocents you saved."

"You are not innocent. None of you are," Elesté hissed. She jerked free of his grasp. "And now... now I am stained by my evil deeds. A death is only fitting for me." She spun around. "Look! Look at the vampire-children I saved."

Drathanyi fixed his eyes on the dark stone city of Druenel-Hai.

A moment's span later, he caught sight of what Elesté referred to—a young vampire boy of no more than ten, feasting on the blood of a blind healer.

"Light burn me! Light condemn me to eternal flame—let justice be done. Goodbye!" Free from Drathanyi's restraining hands, she wedged her foot onto a parapet and flung herself many fathoms to her death.

Though less than half of the army had been within sight of the blinding wand, all the veteran Lamen troops had apparently kept close to the now-bloodless King, while the inexperienced had remained behind the gate. By the time the several thousand had been cut down or drunk dry, and the battle pushed to the forefront of the gaping hole where the gate had been, the Lamen line had already begun to falter.

~

When morning broke over the City of Vampires, and Drathanyi had returned to the wall to reflect in silent contemplation, the light of the sun was unwelcome. In the city square lay a veritable carpet of bloodless white corpses, each drunk dry. Drathanyi's subjects danced in the streets to the sound of pipes and lutes. The Redwine Tavern had brought out kegs of mead. The feeling of joy and delirium had become almost palpable in the air, but Drathanyi shirked from it, trying only to reflect on the great cost by which they had purchased their victory.

In the daylight, he did not stir. The nighttime was when he felt most alive. Drathanyi realized he hated the sun.

Late in the day, a caravan of soldiers appeared in the horizon, following the path distinguished by wooden markers across the snow. Drathanyi knew it was his wife, come from hiding.

"Drathanyi!"

The voice behind him sent chills tearing up his spine. He spun around in an instant, drawing *Lifedrinker*, and met the black eyes of Niamé head-on, even as the *estirion* blade broke the dagger she had thrust forward in two.

Still her eyes burned with inconsolable wrath.

"I should kill you," Drathanyi said. "Gods know, you deserve it. But I will not prove the do-gooders right. Enough people have died today."

Niamé gasped in disbelief as Drathanyi, King of the Vampires, left down the scaffolding to the ground floor.

~

That evening Drathanyi took his seat on the Crimson Throne as the *Drazzandori*, and for the first time, in peace. Niamé's rage had quieted; she stood at the side of her lord Drathanyi and his lady-wife Admé, as she would stand without incident for the remaining seventy years of her life.

EPILOGUE

Never again did the Lamen King question the legitimacy of the druen nation. Never again did the Lonen invade or ally with the Lamen race against the druen.

Never did all nations under sun and moon call the *drazzandori* their lord; but neither did any question his right to rule.

"In the vampire nation, there are no heroes, only villains…"

But all are villains.

"Seeing the great darkness within the elven prince's heart, the High God cursed his descendants with a thirst for blood…"

But against the curse they prevailed.

GLOSSARY

ALL-SEEING ORB

A magic tool, crafted in the prior age, that allows the user to remotely view any location in the world. Three were created. One was lost during the Great War and probably destroyed. One legend states that—when brought together—they allow the viewer to see the past, present, and future.

ANDOMASI MERCENARIES

Mercenaries from Port Andom take much of their martial traditions from the Lonen. They wear heavy armor and wield halberds, as well as crabshell-shaped full helmets. They command high prices in Nardur and abroad.

BLACK ZEALOTS

A group of shapeshifting magic weavers, centered in a base of operations called the Lonely Temple. Their goals are enigmatic and ever-shifting. Not even the druen royalty has full influence over them. In addition to shape-shifting powers, they can rally themselves into a frenzy called an *ecstasy,* by which they make group decisions.

BLOOD KNIGHTS

An order of soldiers in the service of the king and some great lords. They are the heaviest armored of druen warriors, and employ a style of combat that combines traditional heavy weaponry with druen bloodthirst. They wear red surcoats and ride fully-armored destriers. They are trained from a very young age and sworn to a strict code of honor and loyalty. As knights, they form the most heavily armed and armored unit of all druen troops.

BLOOD SORCERERS

A group of Lonen magic weavers with power over blood. They have their headquarters in the Blood Keep, which is located in an isolated forest of the Riverlands. Virtually all male, they often experiment with captive animals and people to create new minions. Their creations include blood fiends and blood elementals. They also create poisons with befouled blood.

DANARION

Danarion, the capital of Lamdar, is called many things: the City of Light (*Lunadarion*); the House of the Gods (*Mitri Danoren*); and others. Among the elves it is known as a sacred place, a hallowed ground; and a sense pervades that, if Danarion falls, there is no hope.

With few exceptions, Danarion is a homogenously elven city. The only non-elves allowed beyond the general district are those designated as elf-friends (*quilenthari*)—a title given to very few.

The city was founded in time immemorial, thousands of years prior to the Age of Humanity (*Xani Vardoren*). It has been the seat of the Lamen kings and the center of the priesthood since unremembered time. Some wonder whether Danarion has always existed.

The Districts

• Quilendon: Non-elves are welcome to this main entrance area. Only elf-friends (*quilentharen*) are allowed beyond. Numerous markets are here. Also notable is the Shrine of Atonement, where penitents can offer coins.

• Peladdon: "The Hill of Fire"—one of the three holy, blocked-off districts of Danarion—is the center of the priesthood.

• Luaddon: "The Hill of Light"—one of the three holy, blocked-off districts of Danarion—is the center of the lightbearers (light-wielding wizards).

• Amanddon: "The Hill of Healing"—one of the three holy districts of Danarion—is the center of the Healers (wizards of renewal). It is open to the public; however, all visitors must wash themselves and don the orange robes of holiness before entering. In the center of Amanddon is the Healing House (*Mitri Amantas*). With exceedingly rare exceptions, only elves are admitted within its doors.

• Viaddon: This garden district has no houses or shops by royal decree. The whole area is a garden dotted with gazebos and fountains. Harpists add to the overall sense of tranquility in this district. Butterflies and colorful birds fill the air in the summer.

• Riadon: "The Hill of Iron" is blocked off to the public. It is in the exact center of the city. It contains the King's residence and a large garrison of soldiers. No non-elves are allowed inside at any time, even elf-friends (*quilentharen*). Here lies the legendary Three Towers which rise high above the skyline: the King's Tower, the White Tower, and the Tower of Warding.

• Hanaddon: The only place where anything resembling vice can be found, Hanaddon is a center of whatever the Lamen Elves despise, within limits. Prostitution is officially forbidden, as it is viewed as a sadness (*moritas*); however, this rule is not enforced within the district. The unsavory House of Mirth is a center of gambling, drinking, drugs, and illicit entertainments. Despite the district's poor reputation, it is agreed by the priests, the lightbearers, and the healers that it is not to be destroyed. Anyone leaving from Hanaddon into an area other than the general district must wash themselves and make an offering at the Shrine of Atonement.

DANTHELON LUNITAR

Danthelon Lunitar, the greatest elf smith, lived in the prior age the Time of the Elves (*Xani Quiloren*), and crafted a variety of wonders such as *estirion*, the hardest metal in existence. He also invented star-gems and crafted a variety of powerful amulets and magic rings.

DARK ONE, THE

The lord of darkness (*maldori*), the enemy of the gods.

DÓ KENTAS

Literally, "The Way of the Staff," *dó kentas* is the elves' most ancient and highly respected martial art. It focuses on mobility, stunning and immobilizing rather than killing opponents, and dodging foes rather than wearing heavy armor. All *dó kentaren* must swear themselves to a rigid code of honor and loyalty to the Lamen King.

DUNDARI

The Queen of the Great White North, a city once subject to Prince Gilden, lies at the northern edge of the inhabited world. One of its largest attractions, a series of hot springs, allows people to stay warm even in the dead of winter. In the Time of the Elves, when the world was warmer, Dundari served as a medicinal retreat and resort.

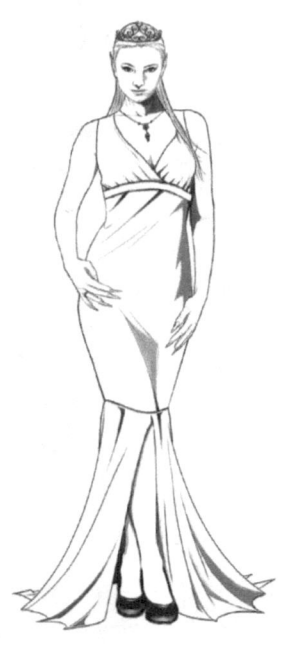

DRUEN NOBILITY

Though there exist some tenuous laws of inheritance and succession, few royal dynasties last multiple generations. When a general or great lord gains enough power, it is quite expected that he will challenge the king.

However, there is a heritage system as well. Druen lords *(drendoren)* rule over their fiefs with an iron fist, with many families retaining control since time immemorial. Wealth and power are never completely out of reach for the non-slave, however, and many merchants and tradesmen have built fortunes in Nardur.

Fashions, such as the spidersilk gown seen in the adjacent picture, are set by the king and queen and filter down through the great lords.

DRUENEL-HAI

The capital of Nardur is the only sizable town in the land of the vampires. Six thousand druen and their slaves live within the stone walls. Built along a river known as Black River *(Nar' Hannon)*, and less than a mile from the frigid, salty waters of the North Sea, it is the initial destination of slaves and the source of any sparse culture and refinement that Nardur can offer. The evil of the legendary City of Vampires is the fodder of scary tales across the world.

From the palace, the King and Queen of the Vampires *(Drazzandori y*

Drazzandoré) rule over the populace. The royal family has an anciently established right of first blood; at their request, the firstborn of any Druenel-Hai citizen may be the victim of the infamous blood-feast.

Despite the dark-hearted nature of the city, measures are taken to retain the people's sanity. History has shown—in the wild "ghouls" of Sardur to the south, and in the blood-crazed, wandering Morthen— that the druen's lust for blood can wreck civilization and order. The blood-feast is performed privately, on threat of death. However, there is nothing altruistic in this rule, no concern for victims; only a goal of order, survival, and self-preservation.

SIGHTS

• The Black Altar: In the center of the town square, an altar of black stone sits unused. Though no sacrifices have taken place in recent memory, its purpose—even if unspoken-of—is clear. The original vampire settlers worshiped the Dark One, and it was here that they offered innocent lives to him. Some consider this monument a matter of national shame; others speak well of the Dark One, saying that sacrifices should begin again, and are not reprimanded.

• The Drusion: Properly known as the Castle of Drusion, and nicknamed the Black Castle, this is the abode of the King and Queen of the Vampires. None are permitted to enter without invitation; any unwelcome guests, regardless of age, fit the rule of right of first blood, and become the object of the royal family's blood-feast.

• Gilden Monument: A statue of black stone, carved into the shape of the first vampire.

• Grand Slave Market: Dozens, sometimes hundreds, of slaves are brought here each day. Many are sold to the outlying villages; others stay in Druenel-Hai. Their fate is inevitably grim.

• The Library of Druthor: A small collection of scrolls and codices can be found here, including (and especially) works banned by the non-cursed elves. It was built by the second *drazzandori*, Druthor the Great (*Druthor Gilthas*).

ESTIRION

The most resilient and piercing metal in existence. An *estirion* sword can pierce heavy iron armor with minimal effort, and an *estirion* mallet can sunder stone like brittle clay. Such weapons are so rare that only close relatives of the Lamen King possess them.

GILTHON CASTLE

The citadel and center of administration for Marlon, the former capital of Londor Province. It was demolished by the King soon after the Prince Gilden's exile.

GREAT WAR, THE

A worldwide struggle between the Dark One and the gods which brought about the end of the Elven Age.

IRON SORCERY

A group of Londoren magic weavers with power over iron, they are virtually always female. The Lonen king values them highly and uses them in battle. They have their base of operations at the Iron Citadel, a fortress layered in iron, in the middle of an island, Iron Isle, in the Eastern Sea. The High Sorceress is their absolute ruler.

KARDIR

The so-called Wild Elves live in a vast plain south of the River Galion, eking out a nomadic existence. They sell pipeweed and aurochs-hides in exchange for iron weaponry.

LAMDAR

The Lamen, or High Elves, are the original Elven tribe from which all the others branched out. They claim their King (*Indori*) alone has the right to rule.

The Lamen at War

The traditional weapon of the Lamen warrior is the quarterstaff. In ancient Lamen history, armor was very light; at most, they wore scale-mail vambraces and greaves. Helmets were sometimes worn; however, the typical image of a Lamen warrior was that of a man with flowing, wild blond hair covered in war-paint.

Though quarterstaffs are the traditional weapon of the Warriors of Light and Life, blades have always been wielded throughout the nation's history. Over time, the Lamen army has grown heavily armed and armored, with an emphasis on swords and long-knives rather than blunt instruments. By the 300s A.H., Lamen soldiers had begun wearing thick breastplates, as seen in the adjacent picture, and quarterstaffs became the exception rather than the rule. Traditional combats, duels and games remain predominantly unarmored battles of the quarterstaff, however.

Lamen armies are notable for the presence of healers. Among the Lamen, magical power is often manifested in renewal and healing. This provides an incalculable asset to Lamen warriors, although even healers cannot bring them back from the dead. In war, the Lamen King often hires auxiliaries: most often, archers of the Umen tribe and Nurnen stag riders. Hiring non-elves is an offense (*naritas*) and forbidden.

LONDOR

From their capital city of Naremon, the Lonen Elves rule the eastern world and, though the Lamen despise it, the so-called "Dark Elves" live free from their grasp.

Religion

The Lonen Elves consider themselves atheists, but others disagree. Their belief in Nothing or Lady Nihil (*Narenté Doré*) is codified to the extent that it has almost become a deity, an entity in itself. Among other doctrines, the Lonen religion claims that morality should be dictated by the monarch and his or her advisors.

War

Londor's troops are, perhaps, the most heavily armored of the elven armies. They often wear heavy mail and full helmets. The most famous of their soldiers are their halberdiers. They are also rare among elves in that—instead of the bow—they use crossbows extensively.

Their wizards often serve in battle. Magic among the Lonen tends to be sexually dimorphic. Among men, sorcerers most often have the power of blood magic and have their center of operations in the Blood Keep east of Naremon. Among women, sorceresses most often have the power of iron magic. The sorceresses have their center of operations on an island off the coast of the Riverlands, Iron Isle, and their citadel the Iron Tower from which the High Sorceress rules. A minority of sorceresses have other powers, such as necromancy.

Society

Unlike the other elven kingdoms, Londor practices slavery. Slaves are often captured from human lands, or from battles with other elves. These are sold to human tyrants, brought back into the Londor Kingdom, or shipped to Nardur, the country of the vampires.

Enemies

The traditional enemies of the Lonen Elves are the Lamen Elves. They have a tense relationship with the Wild Elves of Kardir to the south, having alternately supported or fought with them at different periods.

The Lonen state has—in the moral law it established—commanded that the Lonen armies will not conquer or subjugate non-elven lands. It argues this is a form of kingship, imperialism and domination which the Lonen settlers fled from. However, no such restriction applies to their elven or non-human enemies.

LONGKNIFE

An elven slashing weapon, longer than a dagger but thinner than a shortsword.

MANY FACES OF LIGHT, THE

An elven term for the gods, indicating their unity as facets of the Light (*Illunê*) or the Lord of Light (*Illunaddori*).

MARLON

The capital of Londor, the largest city in the east. Once, the seat of Prince Gilden's realm. At its height, thirty thousand people lived within its walls, but it declined quickly during the Great War.

PRINCE GILDEN

Gilden (6685 A.E. to 15 A.H. or 508-301 Y.B.E.) was the adopted son of King Danthemari IX. He was of uncertain parentage, but entered the royal household along with his sister at a very young age. As a young man he was blessed — along with his sister — with stunning good looks. However, rumors began to surface early on of an incestuous relationship between Gilden and his sister Elloré. King Danthemari believed it purely gossip and ignored it.

King Danthemari appointed Gilden, at age 60, as prince over the province of Londor. His sister, despite Danthemari's wishes otherwise, moved with him to the Londoren capital of Marlon. From the beginning, Prince Gilden became feared for his capricious cruelty. He doubled the tax rate to build himself more and more lavish residences. He took a special interest in the religion of the most ancient elves, before the belief of the gods became widespread. The common people of Marlon called him Gilden the Evildoer (*Gilden Malari*).

At the outbreak of the Shadow War, Prince Gilden officially married his sister Elloré, defected from the Elven Kingdom, and announced his allegiance with the Dark One. He fought tirelessly to keep the Riverlands and other regions under his sway. He besieged the capital of Danarion and surrounded it for 13 days, only to be outmaneuvered and driven away. There, a prophecy was born — words uttered from Prince Gilden's lips, that one of his descendants would massacre the inhabitants of Danarion and leave no brick standing.

At the end of the Shadow War, Prince Gilden found himself in control only of the lands immediately surrounding Marlon, isolated and friendless. Now old and decrepit, he became increasingly paranoid. Suspecting his sister-wife Elloré of conspiring with the new Lamen King Danirias, he killed her with his own hands.

The gods bestowed on both Gilden and his descendants the Vampire's Curse. His descendants, the druen, live on in Nardur and elsewhere to this day.

NON

A land bordering the far north of the Elven Sea, heavily wooded and undeveloped. Her people are known as the Nurnen, or Gray Elves.

<u>War</u>

The Nurnen Elves' best and most common warriors are their stag riders. The domesticated reindeer are sometimes dressed in steel barding, according to the situation. The stag riders are known for their fearlessness and swiftness, and for their devastating charge. The reindeer are swifter than horses, are considerably larger, and can bowl over their enemies with their antlers, a tactic that often devastates enemy cavalry.

Nurnese deer are naturally fearful of non-elves and will run away from them unless commanded otherwise by their master. Only stags, with their fearsome antlers, are used in battle. Stags build an emotional, enduring bond with their riders that some call spiritual. Deer are not killed for venison except in times of famine.

Society

The lord of Non serves the King of Lamdar. He is not given the title of king (*Indori*) but instead War Lord (*Velddori*). The Nurnen are nomads and herders, having little value for towns; however, the ceremonial capital of Non, often lying empty for months at a time, is called Nurnai.

Two things make the Nurnen Elves famous: their stag riders and their spidersilk. Giant spiders live in a cave in the south of Non, and from their gossamer webs, Nurnen Elves weave a special silken cloth (called simply "elvencloth" by humans) which is one of the most valued fabrics in the world.

Enemies

The Nurnen have few enemies; they are surrounded by allies to the east and west, and to the north is an icy wasteland. Their harmonious society means rebellion and infighting is almost unheard-of. They serve the Lamen Elves in war.

PORT ANDOM

Founded by the bandit lord Andomas, Port Andom (*Andomarvon*) is an isolated outpost and the bridge between Nardur and the wider Elven World. It also serves as a transit-point for slaves between the markets of Londor and Nardur. Its main exports are crabs fished from the North Sea, slaves, and mercenary soldiers.

RED GUARD, THE

A bodyguard for the druen king, named for their red cloaks.

RIVERLANDS

The Riverlands (*Hannadoren*) are located on the south-easternmost portion of Londor, where the River Saron meets the Eastern Sea. From the coastal port of Sarderon, several miles out to sea, lies the Iron Isle where the iron sorceresses have their headquarters. Northwest of Sarderon, in a dense forest, lies the Blood Keep where the blood sorcerers have their base of operations.

Geography

The Riverlands are a thickly wooded area, covered in brambles and pine trees. Over time, much of the wetland was drained and the timber was harvested for building or sold to other nations. Much of the region remains heavily wooded, however.

Those wandering the secluded areas of the Riverlands should beware the natural fauna:

• Blood fiends, leftover experiments from the Blood Keep, resemble hulking apes with numerous spider-like eyes and wolf-like claws. Steel swords bounce off their blood-red hides like rubber. Like the druen of the far north, they thirst for blood. Like flies, they lay eggs in carcasses, a small portion of which turn into adult blood fiends. Few can outrun them, and even fewer can fight them off. Attempts to exterminate them have failed, and proven deadly for hunters. The population has only grown.

• Flamepelt panthers, one of the natural wonders of the Riverlands, have coats that change color. The coats turn a burnt red-gold in summer, and pure white in winter. Their sapphire-like eyes are a fiery blue in summer and a pale, whitish blue in winter. They do not naturally prey on elves, but cornered or frightened flamepelt cats will often attack.

RIVER GALION, THE

A river leading west from Naremon into the human realm.

RIVER SARON, THE

A river on the eastern edge of the elven world which empties into the Bay of Iron and the Eastern Sea.

SARDERON

A town built where the River Saron empties into the Bay of Iron. It is constructed on wooden piles driven deep into the marshy ground and navigated via canals. The lord of Sarderon is called a minor lord (*daurion*) in service to the Lonen king but, thanks to the town's distance from Naremon, he has nearly autonomous control over his subjects. It is, by far, the largest settlement in the Riverlands.

SARDUR

A region of mountainous hills south of Nardur inhabited by a crazed variety of druen scornfully referred to as the "Hill Ghouls" or "Hill Cannibals."

SORELDA

The land of a lost Elvish tribe, reclusive in nature, known for their hag goddess and twisted magic.

SLAVERY

Slavery has been legal since the vampire nation's inception. Originally, all slaves were non-druen, whether war captives or unfortunates purchased wholesale from Lonen traders. Over time, some druen became slaves—a phenomenon that only occurred when debts went unpaid. The children of slaves automatically receive slave status. Only the mercy of their owners can set slaves free.

SNOW MEN

Hairy, simian predators of the White Wastes. They live in ice caves and will actively hunt humanoids.

UMDAR

The Umen, or Forest Elves, live in a vast expanse of temperate rainforest on the western edge of the Elven world.

War

Umen are revered as master archers. Unwelcome intruders to Umdar may find themselves—in an unexpected instant—surrounded by bows as the rangers reveal themselves. The Umen are known for their stealth, their ability to move through the forests of the giant spruces without being heard. Among the elves, they are believed to possess the greatest skill with the bow of any people.

Magic among the Umen is sexually dimorphic, like the Lonen but to a lesser degree. Women are mostly but not exclusively treespeakers, having the power to shape and bend vegetation. Men are mostly but not exclusively beastfriends, able to calm and command animals, often enlisting them in war. However, forcing an animal to serve in war against its will is forbidden (*nordas*). The most common use of these allies is surveillance. Intruders in the Umdar forests should beware the woodpeckers and kingfishers: often the birds are the allies of the beastfriends, serving as spies.

Society

The Umen Elves have many nicknames, but one—the Tree Folk—is perhaps the most fitting. Towns are built within trees, supernaturally formed by the Treespeakers. The great pines sometimes reach heights of more than 300 feet. The largest town, Darumi, is built around and within one of these giant trees. The Treeshapers have molded its shape into one proper for a city.

Unlike the humbler Nurnen, the leader of the Umen calls himself king (*Innori*) to the mild irritation of the Lamen King. In most ways the King of the Umen acknowledges his inferior status.

STAR-GEMS

Also called "starstones," these lights are crafted from a white-colored crystal that absorbs magical energy. Lightbearers will infuse the crystal with power and, depending on the skill of the lightbearer, the objects can emit light for as long as a hundred years. The city of Danarion uses star-gems as streetlamps.

VARRENDA

The Elvish term for human lands. Short for *vardorenda*, literally, "the world of the humans."

WHITE DRAKES

Draconic beasts in service of the Lonen king. They were instrumental in the Great War, when the break-away Lonen lords fought Prince Gilden. The White Drakes breathe out a sickening gas that can nauseate opponents, but their most deadly weapons are their teeth, which can crush opponents, armor and all. They serve only the royal family of Londor. Their origins are a mystery and will likely remain so, following the burning of the Royal Library during the Great War.

WHITE WASTES

A vast expanse of snow and ice that runs from the Ever-Ice north of Nardur to the town of Dundari.

YAN

A gold coin, the most valuable unit of elven currency.

ABOUT THE AUTHOR

Cursed at birth with a wild imagination, Andrew Cooper spent his youth dreaming of worlds more exciting than Earth.

He finds inspiration in the epic masterpieces of Tolkien as well as the deeply heartfelt works of Shirley Jackson. He sold his first story at age 19 to a fantasy magazine and attended the Odyssey Writing Workshop in 2010. His stories have appeared in Morpheus Tales, Fear and Trembling, Residential Aliens and Writer's Digest top 100 magazine Mindflights, among others.

He currently lives in Northern Michigan with his family.

CONTACT THE AUTHOR

Visit **www.aj-cooper.com** to sign up for the newsletter and stay up-to-date on new releases.

Find him on Facebook at:

www.facebook.com/AJCooperauthor.